unfinished

stories finished by
lily hoang

black on cream edition

Also by Lily Hoang

Parabola
Changing
The Evolutionary Revolution

unfinished

stories finished by

lily hoang

Jaded Ibis Press
sustainable literature by digital means™
an imprint of Jaded Ibis Productions U.S.A.

© 2010 copyright Lily Hoang

First edition. All rights reserved.

ISBN: : 978-1-937543-04-4

Library of Congress Control Number: 2012947901

Published by Jaded Ibis Press, *sustainable literature by digital means*™
An imprint of Jaded Ibis Productions, LLC, Seattle, Washington USA
http://jadedibisproductions.com

Unfinished cover art by Ella Norton. Finished by Anne Austin Pearce.

This book is also available in digital and fine art limited editions. Visit
our website for more information.

The author graciously thanks the twenty brilliant writers who dared to let me finish their stories. Bios for contributing writers and artists may be found on pages 202-205.

Kate **Bernheimer**
Blake **Butler**
Beth **Couture**
Debra **Di Blasi**
Justin **Dobbs**
Trevor **Dodge**
Zach **Dodson**
Brian **Evenson**
Scott **Garson**
Carol **Guess**
Elizabeth **Hildreth**
John **Madera**
Ryan **Manning**
Michael **Martone**
Kelcey **Parker**
Ted **Pelton**
Kathleen **Rooney**
Davis **Schneiderman**
Michael **Stewart**
J. A. **Tyler**

The author would also like to thank: her family, Steve Tomasula, the fabulous Debra Di Blasi, Frances Hwang, and of course, Karl & the cats.

Previous incarnations of some of the stories in this collection have appeared or are forthcoming in: *Hobart Pulp, The Coming Envelope, Make Magazine, Squid Quarterly, TELL,* and *Re: Telling.*

contents

At the beginning of a story, attack a subject, no matter where, and open with some very beautiful phrases which will arouse the desire to complete it.

– Baudelaire

unfinished

forward

In May 2009, as the summer barreled its way toward me, I began thinking about a book project. I had quite a few short stories started and abandoned, and I entertained the idea of starting a collection, but when I re-examined my forgotten fragments, I couldn't stand them. They were trash.

Then, the idea struck me: If I had abandoned so many stories, other writers must have as well. So I sent out a request to my favorite writers, asking for their scraps, stories or poems they couldn't finish, wouldn't finish, things they'd simply discarded. I offered to finish their stories for them.

Given the nature of this project, I was surprised by the generous and enthusiastic response. In my request, I asked for unfinished stories, which I would then finish. There were no parameters on what they could give me. Some writers gave me pages and pages. These were the most difficult stories for me to finish, as a voice and plot had been established. Most writers, however, gave me anywhere from one sentence to a few paragraphs. Some writers gave me fabulist fiction. This is my comfort zone. With those stories, I played. Other writers gave me realist fiction. With those stories, I struggled more than played.

This has been a collaborative process. After completing each story, I offered the original authors the opportunity to edit, revise, etc. Many of them did. Others didn't. In this collection, I have tried my best to retain the original writers' voice and style to the best of my ability, but of course, they are stories I have co-opted and taken as my own. Common themes and styles do emerge, but more than anything else, this is a collection of other people's carrion, which I have — like

lily hoang

Frankenstein — resurrected. I hope, unlike Frankenstein, that I have more empathy for my created monster than the good doctor did. And, of course, I have emerged alive and relatively unscathed!

Here, you have twenty-one finished stories, started and abandoned by someone else, that I have ended.

Lily Hoang
September 2009

your ballad of milt & stanley

(from Brian Evenson)

So let's just avoid conflict, why don't we? What made you think, even for an instant, that Stanley had a chance with the cool kids? I mean, poor bastard transfers to a new school and what does he wear the first day? Seriously, he comes to school wearing a clip-on tie and a cardigan. A fucking clip-on tie. And now you think he's got a chance with the cool kids just because one day later he's taken off the tie and the cardigan?

That shit sticks with you.

By the time he hits fifth grade, he'll still be seen as a stiff. Maybe when he gets to junior high, the kids might forget about it, but now, right now, it doesn't matter how much gel he puts in his hair or how tall his spikes can get, Stanley's the class square. There's no way around it.

But you, you just can't stop yourself, can you? It's like you're caught in some bizarre musical theatre world where Stanley can transform himself into the greased-lightning cool kid overnight, like he'll come into school the next day, smoking a cigarette and shagging the hottest girl in the class, well, bud, that's just not the way it works. But you can't carry it through, can you? You got so far as to style his hair and dress him in normal kid clothes — hell, let's be generous here. He's even wearing semi-cool clothes — and you march him into the classroom after the bell rings (dangerous!), and where do you have him sit down? You have him sit in Milt's seat. Fuck.

And this is the make it or break it moment, the one that stands in the storybooks as the decisive moment of Stanley's pathetic life. You could have sat him in any empty seat of the whole room, but instead, you put him in the only seat that says, "Milt's motherfucking chair: Don't sit down." Because last year Milt was in this class. And the year before that, Milt was in this class. Milt's been sitting in that one chair for two and a half years — and you put your little homeboy in that seat!

Poor Stanley doesn't even know any better. For all he knows, he's sitting in any seat. He doesn't know Milt. He can barely differentiate the cool kids from the nerds. But you. You know better. You could have sat him anywhere, and now, here it is. Stanley's fucked because Milt didn't skip class today. Milt's just walked into the room, and the whole room's quiet. Even the teacher. Even the teacher who's supposed to be teaching arithmetic knows shit's about to go down, and Stanley is just sitting there like a dope.

So here we are. Either Stanley is going to get up and move and live in constant terror for the rest of his fucking life, or he's going to get his ass kicked. But you don't have the stomach for it, do you? No, you want to turn away. You want to close the book. You're such a fucking loser. I mean, just let Stanley get his ass kicked. Make him stand up to Milt for just one second — make him say some dumb shit like, "It's a free country. I can sit where I want!" — and sure, it'll hurt like hell, and sure, he won't be in with the cool kids, but if he stands up to Milt, even for a second, he'll at least get a little respect from the kids at the back of the class, and he'll for sure be in with the kids who sit in the middle of the classroom because, you know, despite what you think, it's not just the kids in the front (nerds) and the kids in the back (cool). There's kids in the middle too. But no, for you, it's either got to be the front row or the back row. You probably didn't even notice those empty chairs in the middle of the room. You were all caught up remembering Stanley sitting in the very front row yesterday, all by himself, and little bastard couldn't even see the chalkboard. He had to scoot the desk up closer like a real kiss-ass. But no, for you, it's either total success or total failure. That's probably why you never could make it even in regional theatre — the highlight of your life before going into sales was a gig or two at the dinner theatre playing Colonel Mustard who didn't do it in the pantry with a candlestick. Yeah, you couldn't even be the star in dinner theatre. But now you get to be the star. Now, you have Stanley.

Or maybe it's just because you've seen too many bad teen flicks, you know, the ones where a kid like Stanley — some dopey nerd of a kid — tries to stand up to some kid like Milt — the coolest bully in school — and he wins. Maybe you've seen some YA flick where the nerd ends up transforming into the cool guy that all the chicks want, but you know what? Even if Stanley does stand up to Milt, even if he does get away with it for just a minute, when no one's looking, Milt will pass a note, crumpled up into a tight ball, that says, "You're dead, punk," or "After school: Four o'clock" and the rest of the year — for the rest of his fucking life — Stanley's going to live in perpetual terror. And I've got news for you: the moment Milt walked into that room and saw Stanley's shit on his desk and looked up and saw the little punk sitting in his desk, Milt knew. Milt knew he'd have to kick Stanley's ass at least once just for looks. What did you expect? Did you really think Stanley would get away with it? Are you going to turn away now, now that you've ruined Stanley's chances at anything? Yeah, you are. I know your type. You're just going to abandon him. Just like that. Because you know that, like you, Stanley doesn't have balls. You know that, like you, Stanley's doomed. Only he's better than you. You hate him just a little bit more for it.

I guess we should just face it: Milt's got more smarts and more balls than both you and Stanley combined. I mean, yeah, so you're scared of conflict, I get it, but come on. This is a story. For Christ's sake, have you ever read a fucking short story before? This is what happens. Conflict. But yeah, I know your kind. You're the kind of asshole who sees Angelina fucking Jolie in Africa with all those little African babies and your heart cracks, and you just can't stop yourself, can you? You're simultaneously choking back your goddamned tears and hiding your chubby. You disgust me. Besides, even though you're the type who sees Angelina Jolie in Africa and starts crying, it's not going to kill you to see Stanley suffer a little, and quite frankly, it's probably good for Stanley too. What was it your father used to say? Do you remember? You used to hate it. Remember? Your daddy used to tell you all the time. He used to say, "Damn it, boy! How many times I got to tell you? If it don't kill you, it makes you stronger." And here you are. I see you. You're not dead. Whatever it was, it didn't kill you because you're still alive, right? Maybe you don't have very good memories of that time he threw you in the lake by the tree with the family of water moccasin, but you sure as hell learned how to swim that day, didn't you? It's just a story for God's sake. But maybe you don't want a story at all. Do you want a story or not? I mean, you're probably the kind of guy — and I'm just guessing here — who gave up his big dream of becoming an actor to sell electronic supplies at some local electronics store that went out of business when Circuit City or Office Depot moved in to the neighboring shithole town next to your shithole town, and now you're dreaming of getting a promotion to "Electronics Supervisor" at Wal*Mart. I feel bad for you, bud. I know you've been hoping for that promotion for years now.

In fact, you're not just hoping for that promotion. No, that promotion is much more than a promotion, isn't it? I know your kind. To you, that promotion symbolizes the start of a whole new life: a chance to "make it." I mean, in all reality, don't you know this is it? Your life has reached its limit, but in your head, you think if you can just get this one promotion to "Electronics Supervisor," you'll finally have the balls to talk to that housewife, you know which one I mean. I've seen how you look at her. You know exactly when she comes in because you steal the surveillance tapes and watch them in the privacy of your own locked room over and over again. I wish I could say there's no shame in that, but it's not even porn, bud. That'd be way more respectable. This is just creepy. She's just shopping. But yeah, so you think if you get this promotion, you'll be taken off night shift and you could actually see her in real life, in real color, and she'll see you, "Electronics Supervisor," and she'll ask you for help and that'll be it. You'll charm the fucking pants off of her, and then, all of this will be worth it. Except, even though you're lost in some warped reality, the truth of it is you know things will never work with Donna — that's what you're calling her, right?

So instead of really stalking Donna, you can focus on Stanley and how to make his life as sweet as possible, even if it means Milt will kick his ass into next year. You're just hoping little Stanley will have the chance you never had, the chance you lose every day that you're a night stocker rather than "Electronics Supervisor." What was it your old man used to say? Give the little guy a chance? You always thought you were the little guy, right? And then you started to grow, and then you weren't so little any more. I don't want to be rude, bud, but you've been the little guy for a long time now, and I've got news for you: you're not so little any more. I know. I know. Little is metaphorical. Like how you feel like a piece of shit most of the time. That makes you little, and so I should give you a chance. I mean, hell, it's really not your fault you're working as night stocker at Wal*Mart. It's really not. I know it's hard out there for you middle-class suburban raised kids. You're the little guy. You're the ones who have suffered, and so when you see Stanley, you feel for him. You're not looking for a story — not a real story anyways — you're looking for a chance at redemption. You're hoping Stanley will stand up to Milt like you'd never have the balls to stand up to anyone. I don't want to call you a loser, bud, but the fact of the matter is that you're not doing so hot right now, and from my end at least, the forecast isn't brightening up any. Looks like storm clouds for miles. Or maybe it's Stanley I'm talking about. Because when it comes down to it, bud, this is a story.

lily **hoang**

Do you want the story or not? Because I can't spend the next decade stalling. It's now or never. Milt's been looming over Stanley for like a century now. What's it going to be?

Look here, bud, you got it all wrong. Milt's not a bad guy. In fact, he's not so different from you. I know this whole time you've been one Stanley's side. You've seen yourself in Stanley, but you know what I think? I think you're afraid of the Milt you've got inside you. You see, like you, Milt's from a nuclear family — a rare species nowadays — and like you, his dad's a real prick and his mom bakes oatmeal fucking raisin cookies from scratch. Like you, Milt's a failure. Or at least he's doomed to be a failure. It's only a matter of time, and really, once he kicks Stanley's ass, everyone knows he's going to get suspended, maybe even expelled, depending on how many bones he breaks. And his parents have been threatening to send him to some military school for like his whole fucking life, and this is it. You see what you've done? Do you know what happens to kids like Milt in military school? They get fucked. Not literally, of course. Well, maybe. Who knows. But really, kids like Milt, they go to military school and all of sudden, they've got no more spirit. Military school crushes them into submission, and even little assholes like Milt start spitting out sirs quicker than curdled milk. You see what you've done? You've ruined not just Stanley's life but quite probably Milt's too. Are you satisfied? Does it make you feel better about your shit job and your pathetic life to destroy their lives too? And of course, you don't even want to confront the possibility of what you've done. No, you'd rather take the easy way out. Shut the book. Go ahead. Fucker. I dare you. Except now, you're too chicken to even stop reading. Too pussy to go on. Too pussy to stop. Pathetic. Have I said that yet? Just fucking pathetic.

But you know what, bud? I actually feel sorry for you, so I'll give you your story. I guess that's the least I can do, considering what a sorry life you've got. I can give you an escape. Only do you really want it? Or is it too much for you? I can see you cringing from here. I can smell it. Literally. I can smell your motherfucking fear. So go on.

Turn the page. Let's see what happens to Stanley.

Thing is, bud, this is what you signed up for. For a second there, I started to feel bad for you. I mean, I get it that you work a shit job and you — unlike most Americans — actually read books for entertainment, and not just books but real literature. I should be impressed with that, but you're the kind of loser who probably jerks off while watching *The News Hour with Jim Lehrer* because of his stellar reporting skills. Then, you switch channels right before you jizz so you can maybe glimpse a shot of Katie Couric's cleavage. Yeah, I know what kind of guy you are. So I want to feel bad for you. I really do, but when it comes down to it, Milt can't feel bad for Stanley and I can't feel bad for you. It's the natural order of things, see? There's a right way and a wrong way. Didn't you old man ever teach you that one?

And so here's Milt. He sees someone else's shit on his desk, and he's like, "Fuck. Now I've got to kick someone's ass." And I want you to slow down. Will you do that for me, bud? Slow the fuck down because when it comes down to it, it's not in anyone's best interest for you to go wailing like a little bitch about Stanley. He'll be fine. Eventually. I mean, what's your problem? Didn't I just try to explain to you how Milt's the guy you should be feeling bad for? I mean, sure, Stanley's the one who's getting the shit kicked out of him — literally, I think here's some excrement coming out of his ass right now — but when it comes down to it, why should we always feel bad for the victim? Isn't Milt just as much of a victim as Stanley? It's hard work being the bully. It's also damn hard work to fail the second grade two years in a row. Not to mention all the other times he's been "held back." Like really, what do you think that does to a kid's confidence? Of course Milt's the bully. He's got nothing else going for him. Stanley, on the other hand, he's got prep school and college and law school. You know Stanley's going Ivy. Or maybe he'll slum it and go to a top-notch liberal arts college. Guys like Stanley, they're going to make it in the long run. Sure, life sucks while they're in elementary school and middle school and high school — high school's probably the worst — but in the end, by the time he starts his freshman year at Yale or Cornell or Dartmouth, he's going to be a stud. Well, maybe not a stud, but by then, nerds will be cool. Smart will be cool. He'll probably even get laid and his girlfriend will be hot. Sure, she's probably fucking some other guy too, but do you think Stanley really cares? God, you're an asshole. Don't you know anything about Stanley? Of course, he'll care! He'll love her. She'll be the best fucking thing that's ever happened to him, but he'll get over it. All he has to do is survive this, right now. All he has to do is stand up and let Milt kick his ass. Then, he'll blink and he'll be in college.

But Milt, there's no hope for him. You know what Milt's got in his future? He'll probably go work at some local store doing retail — if he's lucky and doesn't end up in prison for raping some chick first. Maybe he'll focus and find something he likes. Maybe electronics. But you know how this story goes, right? Maybe that electronics store will be doing well for a while. Milt will be promoted to store manager. Maybe the owners are pretty cool and want to send Milt to technical school so he can learn more about computers or some shit like that. But then, here it comes. Like you didn't know it would happen. One day, just as Milt signs up for that first class at community college or technical school or whatever, Wal*Mart announces that it's going to open a megastore right there in town, and we both know what happens next, right?

The thing is, bud, it all started right here. It all started because you're a drama queen who wanted Stanley to be cool, because you felt so fucking bad for him that first day when he came in with a bow tie and a cardigan. Because you thought Stanley could be your salvation. Then, you saw Milt, and you knew that Stanley would have to stand up to Milt if he was going to make it in school, if he even wanted a chance to hang with the cool kids, but when it comes down to it, why couldn't you be kinder to Milt? Why couldn't you sympathize with the one character who's doomed to have the same fate as you? Because when it comes down to it, bud, did you really think that you're the same as Stanley? What do you two even have in common? Sure, you were a loser in school, but you weren't a nerd, were you?

No, the irony is that you were a kid in the middle. You were the kid you never wanted Stanley to be because you thought if he was a kid in the middle, he'd end up just like you. That's the funny thing, right, bud? Years from now, long after this story is over, it's the Stanley's of the world who'll be rich. They'll have the hot wives. They'll have the kids who are both smart and pretty. That's the problem with people like you. You never see the big picture. You sit your ass down to read a story, and you just sympathize with whoever the narrator tells you to like. You don't have any autonomy. You don't think critically. I mean, sure, Stanley is going to get his ass kicked, no question about it, but does that mean he's the victim in this whole story? Can you see any further than your own nose?

But you know, I get your point. I really do. The whole point of a story is that you, the reader, ought to be whisked away to some alternate reality where you get to be a passive consumer. You get to live vicariously through the characters. Stories offer people a chance to escape. So ultimately, while reading this story, you actually should have felt sympathy for Stanley. You should have wanted him to sit in the back of the classroom or, at the very least, not sit in the front row. You should have wanted him to stand up to the bully. I'm really not criticizing you for all that. That would be unreasonable of me. After all, I did twist the story to make you feel how you felt. I manipulated you. I mean, you're not really the emotional type. You work at Wal*Mart for God's sake. It is what it is. You can't really have much of a spirit left in you after an eight-hour shift there, can you? And then, you come home to a nice microwave dinner and *The News Hour.*

The fact of it is, bud, that yes, you should have felt bad for Stanley. Sure. No problem. But you took it to a whole new level. It's one thing to want something for the character. Right on. It shows how much you care. But it's a whole different thing once you start taking the characters' lives and futures into your own hands. You're not God.

lily **hoang**

You're not even a writer. You're just a lonely guy who still lives with his mom because his dad killed himself a decade ago but you're still worried about your mom being lonely. And again, that's sweet and shit, but you want to know the truth, bud? Even your mom thinks you're a loser. I mean, she thinks you're a nice son, but even nice sons like you should leave the nest every once in a while. What I'm trying to say is that your mom has been seeing someone — I know, it's pretty repulsive to you and probably a little demeaning that your mom can get action when you can't — and she'd really like to bring him home sometime except your sorry ass never leaves. You go to work and then you go straight home. I mean, I get it that it's a shitty little town you live in, but really, can't you give your mom some space? No, instead, you rush home after work and start reading all these books, and I swear it's like you're a five-year-old girl playing house or some shit because rather than reading the story like a normal human being, you start seeing yourself in every character. I don't want to be a prick or anything — and I get you've got "training" in musical theatre — but do you *really* have to dress up like Stanley while you read this? And again, no offense, but you should know that it's creepy as shit that you changed your Wal*Mart nametag to read "Stan." I've got to be honest, bud, that shit's not right. But let me throw you a bone here, give you the benefit of my doubt, even though you obviously don't deserve it. I mean, really, just take off the clip-on tie. I'm trying to be nice here, ok? Because ultimately, why shouldn't you want to sympathize with Stanley? Furthermore, why should I, the narrator, criticize you for doing what I've actually set you up to do? Am I asking too much of my readers?

And so here's Stanley. He sees Milt walk through the door, and he's no dope. I mean, just because you sat him in Milt's chair doesn't mean that he doesn't realize he's committed some big ass faux pas. Now do you see why Milt's got to kick his ass? Stanley's the kind of little pussy who uses words like "faux pas." He deserves it. And here's Milt walking through the door and for a second, just one brief second,

Milt looks Stanley right in the eye and nods.

See? Was that so bad? All this build up and that wasn't so bad, now was it? I'll be straight with you: I didn't think it was going to be good. I didn't think Milt would be nice. Maybe Milt's not such a bad guy after all. Maybe he's a pretty stand-up guy who's not doomed to go work at Wal*Mart when he gets older. Does that make you feel better? I mean, it sure as shit doesn't change your pathetic life, but at least things are looking up for Stanley. Maybe all your musical theatre shit was worth it. Maybe everything will be ok after all.

Only, wait.

What's that?

Fuck.

You really shouldn't look.

the birthday cake

(from Zach Dodson)

The birthday cake sits on the table. It was placed perfectly, purposefully, with a single knife and a single plate next to it. There is a napkin — square — folded in half to make a triangle. The napkin is a used blue. There is a silver fork on top of the napkin.

There is a single chair. The chair alone seems amiss. It is not in front of the napkin-fork combination. It should be moved.

The table is circular.

Everything seems quite ideal. But the birthday cake isn't in the precise center of the table, which isn't very big. The cake ought to be in the middle of the table.

When he hid, the cake was in the middle of the table. Now, it isn't.

There must be a slant in the floor.

The slant must be fairly substantial.

He had intended for the burning candle to dissect the center of the table. This is now impossible, but the event is not ruined.

He is girlish with anticipation. He wishes he could wet himself with delight.

He sits behind a latched door. The door separating him from the cake denies him visual access to the other room. He hopes nothing has caught on fire.

He is in a room. He should be named Samson. He hates it when people call him Sam or Son.

Or when people add an additional letter to his name that clearly does not belong. The room has only one window. The window divides the room from the rest of the world.

Samson gets up and draws back the curtain — a green plaid exported directly from the 1950's — slightly to peer at the street below. There must be many stories separating Samson from solid ground. Luckily, Samson has excellent vision.

Below, there is nothing but the usual chaos.

Above, there is calm, except the slant in the room holding the cake.

Here, the sun stabs him in the eye.

Samson does not squint. He does not close his eyes or allow the curtain to fall back into place.

After several minutes, he withdraws to his original position: sitting, in a chair, placed three feet away from the door, facing the door.

The room, now that it is absent of sun, is dark. It takes Samson some minutes for his eyes to adjust. For those minutes, he is blind, but his hearing is keen.

Sitting, he tugs at his motorcycle boots. They are out of style, he knows, but these are things Samson follows only to maintain conversation.

His boots are the color of spiders. He wonders if one could train a spider to weave a doily.

There is one under the cake: a doily, not a spider.

And it could be poisonous: the cake, not the spider.

There is something crawling at the space where hair meets bare skin: goose bumps, not a spider. He hopes.

The cake shifts back towards to the center of the table. Samson cannot see this, but it is something he wills.

Earlier, Samson gathered the materials to make the cake. He woke earlier than usual. In order to make a perfect cake, Samson knows, he must not apply icing until the cake has had adequate time to cool. He had to account for cooling time, which he had forgotten about the previous time he baked a cake. The result was disastrous, and last night, he chastised himself before falling asleep. This cake, however, is perfect.

Samson took care to buy only the highest quality ingredients. For example: he used vanilla beans, which he crushed with a small knife, rather than vanilla extract. He likes the way the beans provide a variance in texture. It is unexpected and truly pleasurable.

Also, the beans release a smell that traps itself in the ridges and swirls of his fingers. Even now, hours after he made the cake, it remains. Although: his nose delights in detecting scent.

For example: he used turbinado sugar instead of plain, white sugar.

This is not Samson's home, but he has made himself comfortable in this room, while he waits.

This room is a bedroom. The person who sleeps in this bedroom did not make his or her bed after he or she rose this morning. Samson suppresses his desire to impose order on the bed.

In the bedroom, there is also a digital alarm clock.

It would be much more apt if it was not a digital clock but one that ticks. Things cannot always be perfect though.

Next to the unmade bed, there is a bedside table supporting the digital alarm clock, dogearred books, and a lamp. There is no light bulb in the lamp. Or else, it has burned out.

There is no wastebasket in the room, which Samson finds disturbing. He does not need a wastebasket, but every room deserves one.

There are things that make a room functional: a door, a window (preferably two, but one can be sufficient), a flat surface off of which things should not slide, and a wastebasket.

Every room in Samson's home fits these requirements. Bathrooms are particularly tricky, but Samson installed two small windows to fill the space where one window belongs. This may be cheating, he understands, but small rooms, such as bathrooms, must be given some allowances.

Samson has been sitting in this room for a while now, and he suddenly fears he lit the candle too hastily.

After he lit the candle, the taste of sulfur lingered in his mouth. He has a particularly sensitive palate.

He wants to burst out of the room and blow out the candle, lest the flame burrow down to the edge of its wick, digging into the center of the cake. This would destroy the cake. The cake is perfect.

Samson would be devastated if no one else had the opportunity to appreciate its flawlessness.

He would like to use the word *fierce* to describe the cake, but this word has fallen out of popularity.

In the other room, as Samson feared, the flame is lingering dangerously close to the pristine icing. In fact, the wax already stained some areas.

Samson cannot see this though.

But now, as if some god were magnanimous, there is a knock at the front door.

Samson grins sourly.

It doesn't seem right: there should be someone entering the home, not knocking on its door.

Now, as if some other god were even more magnanimous, a key slides and clicks. A knob turns. Two people enter.

Like Samson, they do not belong here.

They enter, and they do not even notice the cake.

From the other room, Samson hears clothes ripping and slaps and pleasure.

This lasts for a minute or two.

Then Samson smells used sex.

This remains. It does not go away.

Then, Samson tastes satisfaction.

In the other room, they who do not belong spy the cake.

One says: Look! A cake!

From the other room, Samson runs his tongue across his teeth like a xylophone.

In the other room, the other says: I'm starving.

The one says: Look! The table is set perfectly. The cake is precisely in the middle of the table.

From the other room, Samson is ready to piss himself.

In the other room, the other notes: There is one single fork, one single napkin, and one single plate. This is cake is not for us.

From the other room, Samson is yelling in his head: Moron!!

In the other room, the one argues: We've already fucked here. There's semen sprayed everywhere. We may as well eat the cake.

From the other room, Samson's heartbeat regains a comfortable speed.

In the other room, the knife enters the cake.

From the other room, Samson is blind to it all.

so cold and far away

(from Kathleen Rooney)

Ruth props herself on her elbows, her body a diagonal platform. Just as quickly, she collapses.

Above her, there is exactly half a moon, a penny cut in two on railroad tracks. Even though she knows it won't look anything like it does now, she takes a photograph anyway. *Caption*, she mumbles, *so cold and far away*.

Ruth has an entire collection of photographs captioned *so cold and far away*, but she doesn't let anyone see them. She puts them in plastic frames with engraved placards taped to their backs. She stows them in a locked drawer, lest Naomi comes snooping around — as she inevitably does — and finds them.

Ruth first began this collection of photographs the night she slept at the feet of Boaz. After she'd removed his shoes, just as Naomi had instructed her to do, she examined his toes. She said to herself, *So cold and far away*, which she'd intended more as a desire than a description, and snapped a quick shot before he woke.

This is not to say Ruth did not like Boaz. She liked him as much as any widow could like her dead husband's next of kin. Which is to say that she loved him enough to marry him.

lily **hoang**

It was unbearably bright the day of their wedding, despite the heaps of snow. They couldn't dig their way out to get to the church, but they married each other anyway. That night, Ruth fled her bedchamber to steal a glimpse of the stars. Instead, she saw Naomi's silhouette slinking slowly towards Boaz.

Ruth doesn't blame Naomi, but at times, she is resentful.

Ruth doesn't blame Naomi because as long as she is married to Boaz, she is free to do as she wishes, as long as she maintains the guise of marriage. To Ruth, this is the best part of married life: the parties, the dinners, the reasons to don pearls and sapphires. They are simple people, but that does not mean they never indulge in small decadences.

And Boaz is a kind husband. He gives her private quarters. Although hers is a small house, more befitting servants or mothers-in-law, Ruth does not complain. It is an attempt at privacy, but she is unsure whose privacy Boaz is trying to protect more.

Theirs is a complicated love, one that is entirely unfair to judge from exterior walls, and they are a private family, one whose walls extend deep into the night sky.

Ruth doesn't blame Naomi because this was, after all, Naomi's clever scheme. Although Naomi is a woman at the height of middle age, her body and beauty have not waned. In fact, Naomi is perhaps more radiant now than when she was Ruth's age. Her skin is buoyant, her breasts resilient. Her eyes are magnets. But it would not look right, a woman of Naomi's age — much less one burdened with her dead son's wife — to be on the market, unless of course her dead son's wife were to be married off. And so it was Naomi who suggested that Ruth go out dancing, take some French lessons, start working out, and it was Naomi who first knew Boaz, who first guided his hand towards Ruth's thigh. It was misleading, certainly, because Naomi wanted

Boaz for herself. By then, surely, Ruth was devastatingly in love, but she was indebted to Naomi.

The day Boaz proposed, he indulged Ruth in unquantifiable ways: a quick trip to Paris for the most lavish dress, brunch with the Queen of England, a private concert by the Berlin Philharmonic, and of course, a spa treatment. Even then, she was surprised when she found a diamond ring at the bottom of her champagne glass. He thought it was original. Ruth used her hands to cover her smile. It was not that long ago that Naomi's son had used the very same tactic on her. She had found it cliché then, as she does now, but Naomi's son is dead and Ruth is a widow and, by any measure, Boaz is a fine man with fair wealth, and Ruth is not such a fool as to ignore any of these truths.

The night Boaz proposed, he demanded sex, but Ruth, being cunning, demanded that he again indulge her in unquantifiable ways and, once sated, she would give him sex. And so for hours, Boaz pleasured Ruth. For hours, Ruth sighed and hummed, until finally, exhausted from anticipation, she screamed. Then, she used the browned skin of her belly to clean off his face and called in Naomi to return his favor.

That night, Ruth went into the night and looked at the moon. It was large and distorted, more oval than round, a penny smashed by a train. She had never felt so invigorated and disgusted. She wanted to call Naomi a whore. She pursed her lips to squeeze out the sound but could not. Of course, she'd known Naomi was lingering outside their door all night. She knew Naomi was waiting for Boaz. She knew Naomi had been fucking him for months, and so only out of spite, she would not give Boaz what he was already getting from her mother-in-law.

There were lines, Ruth thought, between a wife and a mistress, and if a mistress provides a husband with a certain service, the wife should feel no obligation to provide that same service. Otherwise, there would be no necessity for the mistress.

No, Boaz would not get the same goods from both women, and for that reason alone, Ruth would be her husband's greatest conquest.

And so it was for years and years. Boaz would enter Ruth's quarters early in the evening, when the moon was close enough to touch, and he would pleasure her for hours. Some nights, the enticement of her body would be so keen that he would climax without being touched. Because she would not allow traditional penetration, Boaz would attempt to impregnate his wife by aiming his ejaculate as close to her as possible.

What Boaz did not know was that despite Ruth's shields and pride, it was out of fear that she would not allow penetration. Her first husband — Naomi's son — had died before they had consummated their marriage. Ruth was, in fact, a virgin.

The nights Boaz came and went from Ruth's quarters, she would lie in bed and listen for Naomi. Every time, Boaz would call out not Naomi but Ruth's name. Every time, as her mother-in-law fucked her husband, she would take a photograph when he called her name. On their backs, she inscribed, *So cold and far away.* They are a random assortment of photographs, most of them blurred and dark.

But Ruth loved those photographs as she loved Boaz.

During the day, Ruth had no obligations. She wandered around town, buying this and that. Then, she would return home and read or nap. All that was expected of her was that she dine exclusively with Boaz. It was not too much — he said — to ask of his own wife. And so for breakfast, lunch, tea, and dinner, Ruth would trek to the main house, where Boaz and Naomi lived, to eat with her husband. During those meals, Boaz would tell her about his day, his business ventures, his unconditional love. During those meals, Boaz would explain to Ruth how Naomi was not his wife. Surely, he could recognize his luck in having two beautiful women but what he wanted most was Ruth.

Ruth would listen and occasionally clarify her plans for the day if they conflicted with his.

Naomi was never invited to dine with them. Instead, her meals were brought up to her room, which although it was in the main house, was in a separate wing. Boaz insisted that his room should be shared by no one but his own wife.

Yes, of course, Naomi was jealous. And she did not know how to moderate her jealousy.

There were days when Naomi was so enraged that she would wedge herself into the china closet, just to spy on the married couple's mundane conversation. There were days when Naomi would ravage Ruth's room, looking for proof of infidelity or foul play. There were days when Naomi would gather strands of the married couple's discarded hair and stroke them against her face and stomach. She thought, *Even their hair in better than mine.* Then, there were nights when she would not lay with Boaz, arguing that she is at once his in-law's in-law and his mistress, and although she has at times been content with that, she can no longer tolerate it. Those nights, she would give Boaz an ultimatum, but before she could finish speaking, he would tell her he chooses Ruth.

Those nights, Naomi would laugh at him and say, *Ruth! She'll never be the wife you want! She was my son's wife, and during that time, not once did she touch him. Not even an embrace!*

Those nights, Boaz would laugh back and say, *There is more to love than desire, Naomi. That's why I don't love you.*

Somehow, those nights would end in fucking.

Every morning, Boaz goes for long walks in his garden. He carries a pair of shears with him so that he can collect flowers for Ruth. Even in the winter, even when snow erases any semblance of color, Boaz brings Ruth a bouquet of fresh flowers. It is a small gesture of affection that a husband shows his wife.

Ruth is not without kindness. Although she offers Boaz neither flowers nor jewels, after dinner, she cleans his feet with warm soapy water and rubs them with lavender oil. It is a small gesture of affection. For them, this is more intimate than anything that could happen behind locked bedroom doors.

Ruth takes scores of photographs, many of which cannot be aptly labeled, *So cold and far away.* These photographs litter the walls of the main house. Boaz has each one professionally matted and framed. Even when Naomi wants to escape, these photographs stand as reminders that Ruth will always be first.

For their one month anniversary, Boaz gave Ruth a tripod.

For their one year anniversary, Boaz built Ruth a dark room.

Each day of the month that marks the day of their marriage, Boaz gives Ruth a gift relating to photography. Sometimes, it is something small — a new memory card, a new strap for her camera. Other times, his gifts are more extravagant.

The truth of it is that Ruth does love Boaz. She often thinks her love for him could literally kill her. And that is why she refuses to show it.

This is not say that Boaz has given nothing to Naomi, nor that she does not expect sumptuous gifts.

But Boaz makes sure whatever gift he gives Ruth, he gives one of at least one-third the value to Naomi. He came upon this formula rather arbitrarily, and he rarely speaks of it.

Still, all the craftsmen and jewelers know Boaz and his preferences. As such, whenever he goes shopping, everyone knows to offer him selections in mismatched pairs: diamonds and topaz, necklaces and a pair of earrings. Everyone knows that Boaz will give Ruth the better selection, which she will only reluctantly accept, shyly, as if she were not even his wife, and he will give Naomi the lesser present, which she will wear with pride, as if she were not his wife's mother-in-law and his lowly mistress.

Although Ruth followed her mother-in-law across many lands when her husband died and although Ruth was given the choice — and let the record reflect that she was encouraged to go back to her family rather than stay with Naomi — she did not hesitate.

So long ago, ages ago, Ruth had said, *For wherever you go, I will go; And wherever you lodge, I will lodge; Your people shall be my people, and your God, my God. Where you die, I will die, and there will I be buried.*

She would come to regret this decision almost immediately, but at that moment, Ruth understood that Naomi was a lonely woman, one whose husband and sons had died, one who was left with neither money nor family. So when Ruth told Naomi she would follow her anywhere and be the faithful daughter she'd never had, she'd had no idea what to expect. But this arrangement! This was beyond any reasonable expectation for a faithful daughter.

Then came the day Ruth learned she was with child. That day, she locked herself in her closet and refused to emerge. She pulled her sweaters, hats, and scarves down to the ground and built a barricade. There, she softly sang songs of mourning and death to herself and to her child. Even then, she knew it was impossible. Although her own mother had never taught her, Ruth knew where babies came from, and she had never done the necessary deeds to make a baby.

More importantly, however, Ruth understood that Boaz would never believe her fidelity. He would never trust that this child was his. He would call her a whore, as she'd wanted to call Naomi so many times, and banish her from his home, and Ruth would have nowhere to go. Worst of all, Ruth understood this baby, this child, would restore all authority to Naomi.

But perhaps even worse than the previous worst, Ruth thought, was the essential truth that she was faithful to Boaz, that she loved him immensely, and even worse than all that was that she could never say any of these things to him.

For three days, Ruth stayed in her closet, and those were the first times since their marriage that Ruth did not eat breakfast, lunch, and dinner with Boaz.

The first morning, Boaz waited patiently, unwilling to touch his eggs Benedict until Ruth arrived. The eggs eventually became so cold that when the maid came to remove the dish, the yolk had fully solidified.

For the first time in his entire life, Boaz missed breakfast.

More hurt than concerned, Boaz went about his day. Then came lunch.

Boaz sat at the table, his fingers drumming the hard wood of his chair. He was hungry. He was angry. But he refused to eat.

Then, finally, Boaz realized, almost by epiphany, that something must be wrong. He is a quick one, this Boaz.

That first day that Ruth stayed hidden in her closet, Boaz personally went to the kitchen. In many ways, he was surprised he even knew where it was. Boaz asked his cooks and his servants to prepare the most delicious meal for two and deliver it to Ruth's home. He told his butlers to enter quietly and set up a table and chairs, candlelight, the finest silver. He arranged for a cellist to serenade them. But when they arrived in Ruth's house, they found no one there. Still, they set the table and chairs, the candles, the finest silver. They arranged the meal so that no servants would be necessary and Boaz could have complete privacy with Ruth. Even the cellist was instructed to perform in the main house and speakers were set up at the foot of the table, so to provide mood without being obtrusive. It was perfect. Boaz had not forgotten even the smallest detail. Except, of course, Ruth.

When Boaz arrived, he did not knock. He simply entered, as though expected. Boaz was surprised that Ruth was not there, not eager and anxious to see him, ready to wet his face with kisses. He walked through the house many times, which was not difficult because the house was rather compact. Boaz was angry. For Ruth, he'd endured many blows to the ego. but this, this was unforgivable.

Then, again, almost by epiphany, he searched the closets, and there, he found Ruth, sleeping under a pile of sweaters, her hand clenching a large stack of photographs. Boaz was the first and only other person to see these photographs, each with an engraved placard taped to its back that read, *So Cold and Far Away.* Although Boaz could not make out what many of the photographs were, others were recognizable.

And then he knew Ruth loved him, even if she could not say it herself.

Of all of this, Naomi knew nothing. That morning, Boaz had handed her a wad of cash and told her to visit the ocean for a few days of relaxation and pampering. He had not specified which ocean, which gave Naomi free reign. For months, she'd been feeling a steady suffocation. She wanted to run away. She was tired of Ruth and her antics. She was tired of being treated like some cheap whore, and even though Boaz would never treat a woman this way Naomi often found herself wondering whether he thought of her more as mother or mistress.

To Ruth, she was a perpetual mother. To Boaz, she was a mistress on demand. It had grown so hard for her to play chameleon constantly.

So, the morning that Ruth locked herself in her closet, Naomi packed her bags and had the chauffeur take her as far away from land as he could. She knew nothing. That morning, Naomi unfettered.

Because Ruth would not come out, Boaz brought food to her, and together, in the closet, they picnicked over sweaters and scarves. In those dark, tight confines, Ruth talked constantly, openly, about everything except the reason why she refused to re-enter the world.

For three days, the married couple stayed hidden in Ruth's closet. The servants came and went with food, water, wine, fresh clothes. Only occasionally, Boaz would have to take a business call of the utmost importance, but Ruth remained nuzzled at his side so he could not consider it work. Hidden in Ruth's closet, Boaz believed that he was truly the luckiest man in the world.

But soon they would have to emerge. Both Ruth and Boaz understood this.

After three days Ruth opened the closet door, crawled out, and stretched her legs and spine several times before standing. Boaz, with sleep still sealing his eyes, motioned for her return. Then Ruth said, *Boaz, I am with child. It is your child. I have not been unfaithful. I am your wife, and I will be the mother to your child.*

Later Boaz would come to understand what an occasion this was, but right then he merely responded, *I love you.*

Of course, Ruth was disgusted by this cliché, but she whispered, lightly, into his ear, *I love you too, Boaz.*

Then she divested herself and offered Boaz her virginity.

She took a picture of the spots of blood on her sheets, and her husband engraved the placard.

Together, they taped it to the back of the plastic frame and kept it hidden in a locked drawer, lest Naomi came snooping, as she inevitably would.

The day Naomi returned from her visit to the ocean, she was no longer mistress. That day, she learned of all she had missed. That day, she sighed to herself, *Grandmother.*

Because she can no longer be mistress or mother, Naomi asked to name the child.

Ruth had been partial to the name Bernard. Boaz had preferred Pauline or Harold.

But the day Ruth gave birth to a healthy baby boy, they held up the child to Naomi who clearly and articulately said, *Obed.*

And so Ruth begat Obed, who begat Jesse, who begat David — David who would become the greatest of kings.

the whore's machine

(from Debra Di Blasi)

Or else: Where is the line in the dust across which we dare not step?

Assuming: There is a line in the dust, and we dare not step across it.

Assuming: We think collectively.

"This life," she says, as if so sure of another, "takes it out of you."

That's it. That "it." That perpetually reappearing *it* to which we're obliged.

Oblige isn't the right word. Honor. We meant: That perpetually reappearing *it* in which we honor. Yes, that's much fitting.

Suffice to say: she is not part of us.

We challenge her, "If you see the line, step across it."

Here is what separates her from us: dissatisfaction (we feel none); obligation (she feels none); and her ability to see the line in the dust across which we dare not step.

It is unfair that she is the one who can see the line that we cannot see.

Her bones crack and crust. Her blood is full of mold. Here, there is injustice.

Our life is not difficult. She is the only one among us to think it is. She does not belong with us. She brings us down. Our life does not — as she laments — "take *it* out of you." And even if it does, the *it* that our life takes out needs to be extracted. When *it* is extinguished, we function. We produce. *It* is our savior.

We have no formal name for *it*, but we all know the power of *it*. Our scholars once tried to give *it* a title beyond such a vague pronoun, but no word seemed adequate. The replacement words did not glide through our tongues in the necessary manner. When we attempted to swallow these replacement words, we spit them back up whole, no matter how much time had elapsed. When we took these replacement words to be dissected, they refused separation. We could not even learn what made these particular replacement words inadequate.

So we decided by consensus to continue using "it."

We believe *it* refuses to be named.

We respect what *it* desires. We do not struggle against *it*.

Once, a very long time ago, long before we were able to manipulate our bodies to consume words instead of grains and leafy vegetation, long before our philosophy became sophisticated, a woman came to us and bartered. The woman offered us a machine that could translate work into a hardened material, which we could then use as a medium to trade goods and services.

We called her: villain, cunning deceptress, whore. Now, she is known simply as the whore.

But, in the end, we purchased her machine.

In exchange she asked us for a certain amount of land. She took a stick and dragged it around the outskirts of our country. In truth, she did not ask for much land, no more than an acre or two. She left us two ports along the ocean and three entry points to lead us to adjacent countries.

She asked that we never enter her land, no matter what beauties and promises we see.

This seemed fair. Our foremothers and fathers entered into a verbal contract with the whore.

But it has been centuries since the time of the contract. The line the whore drew is no longer visible, yet we must honor it.

This has never been problematic. In fact, if anything, we continue to migrate towards the interior, folding in upon ourselves, building up instead of out, so that we do not disturb her. We do not mind this. It is what is necessary.

It has been so long since the time of the whore. Why do we still fear her and her line?

Assuming: The whore or her begotten still exist.

Assuming: It is out of fear that we do not cross the line.

When she who does not belong speaks, we hate her. We want her to disappear. We want to offer her to the whore, even though the whore has never asked for sacrifices.

Or: Why do we hate she who does not belong?

Or else: Why does she who does not belong not belong here?
Assuming: We do hate her.

Assuming: She indeed does not belong.

We do not know how she who does not belong first came to us. We do not remember her being born, and we do not allow immigrants. Our borders are firmly secured, even along the edges of the ocean.

Although it is possible that she traveled across the whore's land to arrive here. This would certainly make her a whore as well, for all those who have touched the whore's land must also be whores.

There are those among us who claim to have raised her, bore her from their very vaginas, allowed her to suckle at their words. They are not to be trusted either, for we do not remember this. Our memory only accounts for her as a grown woman: one who does not appreciate our barter system; one who complains perpetually and is malcontent constantly; one who we find crystalline in beauty.

We have heard that the whore was also this beautiful.

Not that we are saying that she who does not belong is the whore.

Although she *can* see the line that none of us can see.

Our people are kind in nature. We do not go picking fights with our own kind, or any other kind for that matter. We are peaceful. We have never warred.

The only time of conflict in both our recorded and oral histories dates back to the years directly before the whore appeared. This was a time of great turmoil for us. *It* was unhappy with us, although we did not know why. It is said that the elders of our great land said that it was because we were not working hard enough, because we were not expelling enough of *it*. Our bodies became tainted with *it*, and we could not function.

When our bodies attain too much *it*, we cannot swallow. Although we have never seen it, there are photographs and diagrams attesting to this truth. When our bodies build up too much *it*, we die of starvation, unless we can muster the strength to work until exhaustion. Then, some of *it* may be released, allowing us to swallow bits of broth or applesauce.

During the time of great turmoil, many of us stored an excess of *it* in our bodies. We were weakened. Then, according to our recorded and oral histories, *it* brought forth storms of enormous proportions. All our housing was destroyed. Rods of thunder and tips of tornadoes ripped apart our machines.

Then, a piece of hail that would not melt dove into one of our homes. It held the scent of cardamom and some herb long extinct. How do we know the scent of death?

The home held a family. We allowed the family to determine our future: the scent of death wandered through our land.

We knew we had to kill the family.

But not everyone wanted to. Many of our people argued that smell alone cannot determine death.

We argued that it was not the smell so much as the hail that would not melt.

They argued coincidence.

We argued that there had been many deaths. Something must be done.

They argued that killing was not an answer.

We killed them anyway.

We learned the scent of death. We learned the lesson *it* wanted us to learn.

Days later, the whore arrived.

Chronology is irrelevant. What is certain, however, is that the day the whore arrived, she offered us a machine — in a time when all our machines were broken — and a solution.

Since the time of the whore, there have been no fights or misunderstandings. We maintain words such as "fight" or "misunderstanding" as marks of our evolution, our development. Conceptually, we can comprehend the definitions of these words, but we have not experienced them personally.

This does not mean we are any more lenient on she who does not belong. Although we have developed great capacity for both empathy and sympathy, she who does not belong challenges our very existence. She makes us angry.

But: We have never felt anger. How do we know it is anger we feel?

Or else: We call it anger, but could it not be love, sacrifice, or despair?

Assuming: Our language accounts accurate portrayals of emotions we have never felt.

The thing about she who does not belong is that for so long, we have accepted her. We have made her part of our families. We have invited her to dine with us, to sleep in our homes, to share.

Also: Our lives leave us no room for complaint, and yet here she is, complaining.

She says, "We shouldn't have to work like this."
    We don't understand what she means. There is no other way.
    She says, "Why do we work like this?"
    We work this way because it is the way we work.
    She says, "Why do we not rest? Why do we not take breaks? Why do we not vacation?"
    We have never heard of this word "vacation." It sounds fatal. It sounds like "plague," which we have also never experienced but there is rumor that other countries far away have plagued.
    She says, "This life takes it out of you."
    We say, "Then leave."
    She says, "And where will I go? What will I do? This is my home."
    We don't want her here.
    She says, "If I go, who will operate the whore's machine?"
    She practices a certain logic. That much can never be questioned. She is the only one who can work the whore's machine. Because of

she who does not belong, we trade and barter. She who does not belong is valuable.

See: In our land, each person has a particular position. Each person serves a purpose. It is because each person fulfils her role that we can think and speak in unison. It is because each person works to make a whole that we do not have conflict.

See: This is why she who does not belong has become a problem.

She says, "Who will work the whore's machine?"
    We do not know why we entrusted such a valuable operation to she who does not belong, she who does not have proof of lineage. We are too trusting.
    We call her, "Fraud!"
    She says, "If I run, you will chase me."
    We reckon this is true.
    Or: We will simply let her run. We will let her leave.
    She says, "If you chase me, I will make you cross the whore's line, which you cannot see but I can."
    We think if she ran, we would not chase her.
    Assuming: There was someone else here who could work the whore's machine.
    There is no one else.

We say, "Let us negotiate."
    She says, "You will believe that I belong."
    This is not a possibility, but we do not know to obscure truth.
    We say, "This is not a possibility, although we will try."
    She says, "You will accept me. If you do not, I will run. Then, you will need to chase me. If you chase me, I will take you into the whore's land. Then, she will punish you."
    We say, "We can only try."

She says, "This is not a negotiation."
We do not know exactly what "negotiation" is.
We say, "What else?"
She says, "From here on, I will continue to work the whore's machine but only if we work only three hours a day."

This is not possible. If we work three hours a day, our days must necessarily shrink as well.

Or: Perhaps we can trick her.
We can elongate one hour to equal five. Then, surely, we can work only three hours a day.

But we have never used trickery before. Not even once. We are not sure it works.

She says, "We will work only three hours a day, but those three hours will be not be wasted doing menial things such as talking or reading unrelated materials. We will work three hours a day, but they will be three full hours, without distraction and irrelevance."
This is not possible.
She says, "Three hours of focused work will be the equivalent of our current fifteen hours of tired, exhausted work."
But: What will we do with all this additional time?
She says, "Those are my terms."
We say, "*It* will not be happy with this. We cannot do what *it* deems improper."
We possess a certain logic as well.

She who does not belong stands facing the water. There is a small strip of land separating her from the ocean. One hand sits atop the whore's machine. It is old and very simple: a rusty handcrank, some engravings on the box, a slot for the output. We have never seen inside the whore's machine. It is magic. The whore is a cunning witch magician.

Water licks the edges of land that is not ours.

the man & his treasure

(from Justin Dobbs)

The man is never going to let loose of the treasure he possesses. It is a treasure unlike any treasure he has ever known. It is unlike any treasure anyone he's ever known has ever known. It's a special treasure, which the man knows, and knowing, he can let no one else know, or they will come and connive their way into this treasure that is rightfully his.

The man has many clever ways of hiding his treasure. He has constructed compartments in his garments, so that his treasure is always close to the body, although it should never touch the flesh.

There is no particular reason why his treasure should never touch flesh. It is the man's rule. It is necessary.

He puts on gloves when he transfers his treasure from one hidden compartment to the other.

The man has built a compartment in all of his undershirts where it falls at the small of his back. He has built a compartment in the lining of his silk and his corduroy jackets. In all of his pants, there is a compartment at the base of inner-right ankle. When he is feeling particularly dandy, he has created one for his hat.

The man is not particularly smooth when he transfers the treasure.

The treasure creates a small bulge. The man is not adept at hiding treasure.

But the treasure remains safe nonetheless.

On the train ride to work, the man keeps his treasure in the jacket of his suit. The man yawns. He checks his watch by lifting the cuff of his sleeve. He does a crossword puzzle. There is always a little girl at the same spot outside the train, always playing in a mound of dirt and dust. After he sees the girl, the man lets his eyes drift into sleep. He keeps his hand over the spot where his treasure is hidden beneath layers of cloth.

The man could be a clock. He is that predictable.

Most men on this train are.

He is nothing special, except for his treasure. His treasure makes him more precious than one in a million.

Knowing this, the man tries to seem as normal as possible.

Before the treasure, the man was any other man. Now, this is no longer the case.

The man often thinks that his life has become more tedious with the treasure, not that he minds.

Because he doesn't want to be noticed, the man routinizes his life. Everything he does, he does as casually as possible.

A yawn is exaggerated in its normalcy.

As a consequence, although he hates his wife and his children, he stays with them. He comes home to them every night and eats the creamed chicken his wife prepares for him. He sits at the table looking at his ugly children and his ugly wife and shoves creamed chicken into his mouth. A daughter attempts to say something clever, to which he smiles condescendingly. She is not very smart.

After dinner, the man sits in front of the television while his wife uses her fat hands to wash the dishes. She brings him a frosty beer. She never buys him the right brand, but he drinks it anyway.

He takes out the trash.

He gets up on time every morning.

He takes a quick, cold shower.

He shaves.

He takes his cold, runny eggs with his coffee and juice. His wife doesn't know how he likes his coffee. She always gets it wrong, but he doesn't complain. There is no small talk. Then, of course, the man gets into his car that takes him to the bus that takes him to the train that takes him to work.

Every day — except Saturdays and Sundays — the man arrives at work before the others. He walks by the coffee maker but does not make coffee. Instead, he goes straight into his office and closes the door. There, he puts on a latex glove — he keeps at least three unopened boxes in a locked filing cabinet — and transfers his treasure from his coat to his undershirt. Then, he throws the dirtied glove into the trash bin, tucks back in his shirt, loops his belt in place, buckles it, and sets his left hand on his chair to steady himself.

The man looks at the desk in front of him.

Behind him is a window that overlooks a canal and a courtyard that is surrounded by apartment buildings. If he squints, the man can see a woman undressing. The man looks at his desk. There's a thick report on his desk, written in Courier font, which he dislikes on principle. Beside it, there is a note printed on purple paper, which he looks over without intentionally reading, a bottle of aspirin, and a telephone.

The man sits down. He pushes his spine against the back of the chair, so he can feel his treasure. There's a slight pain to it, the treasure having some sharp edges and all. The man finds it pleasurable.

Then, right on time, his secretary bursts in without knocking — she never knocks and the man wants to remedy this, except it would seem aberrant now that she has been acting this way for years — and asks if he would like a cup of coffee, which she has just brewed.

She says: No, I'm not joking. Would you like a cup of coffee?

The man does not know why she would think he thinks she is

joking. There has been no laughter, not even a smile or a hint of friendliness in their interaction this morning.

The man says: Yes, of course, and maybe a doughnut, if there's any left.

The man always says this, fully knowing the doughnuts have not yet arrived.

His secretary says: Oh well, of course. I'll get right on it.

His secretary mockingly salutes him. Again, the man doesn't laugh or smile or show any hint of friendliness, but she has done this every day for years. He doesn't know why she would continue.

On Saturdays and Sundays, the man still goes to the office, although he must make the coffee himself.

Barring, of course, the possibility that she too has a treasure hidden somewhere that she wishes no one else would know about. The man considers the possibility that she too does not want her actions to seem abnormal. The man looks her over for bulges in inappropriate places but sees only tits and ass.

His secretary winks at him.

He does not respond.

Sometimes, the man reaches back there and pretends to scratch an itch.

Right on time, the secretary bursts right in and hands him his coffee and doughnut.

Unlike his wife, his secretary knows exactly how he likes his coffee.

The coffee is very hot and mixed with hazelnut-flavored cream and almond extract. The secretary buys the almond extract just for him. The doughnut is round and made of chocolate. It is the doughnut he most wanted, and his secretary has satisfied his every need, his needs and wants being mutually interchangeable.

While eating and drinking, the man opens a drawer and pulls out an envelope, and in the envelope, he puts the paper he'd written the day before, and then he picks up the phone to call in his secretary. He has chocolate on his upper lip.

The man drinks his coffee. Outside his window, there is a crane moving over the new apartment building, which is made mostly of brick and glass. Beside that new building is a smaller building — a restaurant — specializing in seafood, which he has been frequenting lately because the food is consistent.

The secretary does not always burst in.

Sometimes, when the door is left ajar, she hovers in that open space, waiting for the man to call her in.

There is a lesson in here somewhere. But who will learn the lesson? It's impossible to tell from here and now.

The secretary looms in the open space at the mouth of the man's office. Most of the door obscures her, but she is not unseen. The man manages to ignore her. While she stands there, uninvited, he reads the report that is sitting on his desk. It is easy enough to read, so he reads it without pause. He flips pages with one hand, drinks coffee with the other. Periodically, the secretary jots down his mumblings. It appears she is taking dictations.

Although the secretary is a roadblock in the middle of the doorway, other employees continue to open and close the door, moving in and out of the man's office. The other employees work in the factory the man manages — or rather the man is a part of management, although he does not own it, nor does he manage it alone. There is much business that must be quite essential in the office, as many employees enter, stay a while, then leave, smiling.

There is nothing suspicious about this. The man is high on the food chain, which is funny because he has been eating a single doughnut for most of the morning.

It could be expected that he would call employees into his office.

Only the man does not call them into his office.

The employees come into his office because he is a kind "suit." He never tells on them and allows them to do whatever they choose in his office, although there is a version of taxation in that if his door is unlocked, he is inside, and if he is inside, he is allowed — by virtue of being a "suit" — to watch and participate, if he so chooses.

The man — in an attempt to be as casual and unobtrusive as possible, lest others suspect he has the treasure — is pleasant towards those who chose to come into his office, even when they have no business being there. It first happened a few weeks after he'd discovered his treasure. He had not yet learned to build compartments in his clothing. At this point, he'd simply put it in his briefcase, beneath a layer of semi-important, necessary papers. One employee came in. He was a line-worker, no one particularly noteworthy to the man. The employee complained of pain caused by repetitive motion.

The form the employee needed to fill out was in the briefcase. The man did not know what to do, so he simply sat there. He told the employee to rest a while. There: on the very lush, ergonomic couch. The employee eventually fell asleep, during which time the man put on a glove, which he'd stashed in his drawers, and removed the treasure from his briefcase and put it in shirt pocket. Although it was hot, the man put back on his suit jacket, to make the treasure seem less protruding. Then, the man transferred his treasure into his pants pocket, although it made an even more impressionable lump there. The man thought: This will have to do for now.

The employee napped until it was time for him to leave. He cleverly forgot to sign the papers necessary for him to get medical attention, thereby allowing him to begin working again.

The next day, the employee arrived at the man's office before the man arrived. Flustered, he allowed the employee to nap again because again, he'd put his treasure in his briefcase.

That day, the man devised a series of secret compartments for his clothes. The employee spread the word that this "suit" was a good one, and other employees began to enter his office for rest and other miscellaneous activities.

There are three couches in the man's office. Originally, there was only one, but the man asked his secretary to buy more and arrange to have them delivered. The man did not want his employees not to have a space when they came into his office. Somehow, his office expanded to accommodate the increased furniture. His office never felt crowded.

Sometimes, the employees would sit or lie with a pillow, or even a blanket if they were particularly tired, all of which the man provided. Sometimes, they would even kiss each other if they wanted to, and the man never complained about it. Sometimes, they would rub each other's crotches with various objects, including their own crotches, and the man would mimic their behavior.

The man watches without watching. He is a busy man, filled with appointments and letters to write, calls to make, so on and so forth.

It is the man's office. He can do as he pleases.

But he does it only to seem natural. He does not want to stick out and make others suspicious of his treasure.

Before lunch, the man transfers his treasure from hidden compartment near the spine of his undershirt to the hidden compartment in the lining of his corduroy jacket.

During lunch, the man goes to the restaurant with the seafood, and he sits behind an aquarium in a dark corner next to a mysterious door. The door says: Mysterious Door. Do NOT Enter.

He nibbles on garlic bread from a bottomless basket and drinks Pepsi from a bottomless glass. He looks at the fishes. He thinks: How are they any different from my employees?

The man does not include himself in this category. Before the treasure, he would have, but not any more.

Remember: the treasure is tucked in the man's corduroy jacket.

It is unseasonably warm inside the restaurant so the man removes his jacket and puts it on the seat across from him.

The man looks at the empty seat across from him. Here, now, the man sees how very alone he is. Even though he has his treasure, he has shared it with nobody. He once thought of showing to his children, but their hands were unpredictably dirty and too small for gloves. He's never considered sharing it with his wife, although when sexual intercourse is required, he thinks of his treasure while fucking her. Without that aid, he is sure he would never reach orgasm. Nor would his pecker be peppy enough for the challenge.

The man considers his secretary worthy of looking at the treasure, but she should never touch it. Of course, the man knows that once seen, the natural desire would be to touch it, which he could never allow.

While eating his bottomless basket of garlic bread, the man realizes how very lonely he is. It is a great burden, that of holding a treasure.

Just then, the mysterious door opens and a mysterious woman emerges. The man thinks: She is a chameleon. Look how she dresses as the other waitresses dress.

The mysterious woman sits across from the man. Her body hides the man's treasure.

The man thinks: This is it. She is the one.

The mysterious woman says: I have been watching you lately and you look so sad. Are you tired? Overworked? I'm overworked. I'm always overworked.

The man thinks: She speaks!

The mysterious woman says: I'll be right back.

The man is flustered. He does not know if he should grab his jacket and flee or stay. He is frozen.

The mysterious woman turns around twice, and in her hands, she holds a cup of coffee. It has hazelnut-flavored cream and almond extract in it, in just the right proportions. She is a mixture of the most beautiful woman he's ever seen and his secretary.

She says: This ought to help.

She says: What's your name?

The man drinks the coffee in one long breath. Then he says: I have to go. But will you be here tomorrow?

The mysterious woman says: You know where I am every day.

The man reaches into his silk jacket to remove his wallet. His hand scratches the treasure. He doesn't mind the blood.

He puts enough money on the table to cover his bill and tip.

He returns to the office, where his secretary will have dressings ready for his wound.

At the end of the day, the man is the last to leave the office. He uses a pass to enter the subway that takes him to the train, that takes him to the bus, that takes him to his car, that takes him home. When the man walks through his front door, there is his fat wife, waiting with creamed chicken, and his ugly children, screaming to tell him about their day.

eight ball

(from Scott Garson)

We had jobs at an old department store downtown, between 7th and 8th. We worked late, not late like bars are open late, more like closing department stores late, which is still late but not that late. We were the closers. We had roughly two hours to ourselves — two hours of silence after a shift of nagging and interrogations — alone in our separate departments. We cleaned, counted tills, made deposits, and so on. No sweeping or vacuuming. There was a whole different crew for that. They came in hours after we'd gone. Once, we tried to wait for them, but Zane got sleepy so we took off.

Kyle was in Men's Wear. He dressed in three piece suits and shining oxblood wingtips. He was like a businessman — smart but conservative haircut, boyish face, royal eyes. Like a perfect doll. He had something of a New England accent, though he was from South St. Paul. We're full of illusions.

After hours, the whole department store turned into an oversized dollhouse. In a way, we had roles. Kyle was Father, just come home from a day on Wall Street. There being only three of us, I was Mother, I suppose.

After hours, all you can hear is the sound of register tape, the occasional footstep on waxed tile, the flutter of garments being shaken. It's like a ball, people dancing in slow motion.

Zane worked in Books. Unlike Kyle, he always wore a rumpled

oxford — white, yellow, or blue — and the same maroon tie, whose pattern of hexagonal mazes resolved to a well-known secret message: Fuck you. Fuck you.

Zane liked to think he was better than all the customers and most of the other employees, me and Kyle excluded — though I think he may have secretly despised Kyle for looking too much the part.

Zane wanted to make movies, which, in some technical way, is what this story is about.

Me: I worked in Lamps. I'd learned some fancy terms — harp, for example; finial. But a lamp is a lamp. People either like it and buy it or they don't. I couldn't technical-support anyone into a purchase. That was clear. I couldn't upsell anything. It's a fucking lamp.

I was paid to wear dresses and be friendly to people if that was what they looked like they wanted. It was my job to guess. I was paid — not that much but probably more than I deserved — because I was young and educated. My boss said that those were appealing qualities in Floor and Table Lighting. My boss was fat but not balding. He had a head full of dandruffy hair and always wore shiny black suits. Bad idea. He liked me because he thought he'd be able to feel me up or something, but nothing like that ever happened.

After I ran through my relatively simple slate of closing chores, I'd lean on the counter to get off my feet. I'd read people like Barbara Kingsolver, long novels that weren't too dumb but didn't require thinking either.

Adele, they'd say — Kyle and Zane — after they'd finished in Men's Wear and Books.

This was ritual. They waited as I crossed the carpeted floor and toed the round buttons, one by one, to darken each station of lighting. They watched. I never got to see the show.

The movie Zane wanted to make was about people just like us — two guys and a girl — and for that reason, I easily cracked myself up asking, What happens? What happens to them?

Even richer was that Zane himself wouldn't laugh. He was geerally pretty nutty. But about his film he was ardent and grave.

I'm sorry, I'd say if I couldn't stop laughing. And the way he'd look at me then, I'd get the idea that I really should be sorry — and maybe I'd say it again.

This was always confusing. I didn't have anything to apologize for with Zane and wanted to slap myself for caving. Still, I could feel bad. I could see Zane seeing me and start to feel honest regret that I was proving to be less than the person he saw.

If I wasn't the Mother in the department store, I was the Daughter, or Girl Next Door. And Zane: the bold, beautiful Son.

Maybe I wanted to think he was some kind of mystic, that his film really would be my fate.

We were out at a bar, drinking, of course. Kyle stood up in the booth seat and took snapshots with his cell. As he did, he asked questions, and so did I — because Zane was trying to conjure the film.

I had the idea that Zane had the idea that Kyle's questions were part of a pose of some sort, that in fact he was more of a listener, really. I thought that Zane might be annoyed with him, slightly. But I wasn't sure. I'd met them outside the department store one night just a month or two earlier. It had been cold; we'd been waiting for the bus.

So the guy…
    Which guy?
    Doesn't matter.
    Which one though?
    Guy #1. Good? Guy #1 finds an eight ball.
    Is this a drug movie?
    No, a billiard ball.
    A billiard ball?

An eight ball. He finds it in the mud.

He's digging?

He's not digging. It's just there in the mud, half buried. The guy sees it, picks it up. He wipes off the mud with a rag.

A rag? Dude carries around a rag in his back pocket or something? Just in case he finds a dirty eight ball?

No. Listen. He wipes off the mud with a rag, which he gets from his car, because he's walking to the car when he finds the eight ball. Get it?

His car.

Yeah, he's headed to work.

Where's he work?

Doesn't matter.

Of course it matters.

Some place like we do. It's not really part of the film.

How can place not be a part of the film?

I'm telling you.

All right, an eight ball.

He wipes it clean. Grips it. Lets it drop to the open cubby between the emergency brake and the gear shift, where it rolls, tocks each of the four plastic sides as the guy makes right and left turns. See?

See what?

It's like a symbol.

I'm holding my tongue!

Or no — a potentiality. An indication to viewers: this guy will be put in play.

So what happens?

I was laughing hysterically by then. Zane was shaking his head. I don't know yet, he said. I don't know.

Even with his teeny cell phone lens, Kyle was talented.

My laughter was golden and blurred, festooned in neon trailings.

Zane and I took our breaks together when Kyle wasn't working. One night, he toyed with a Jefferson nickel on the tabletop as we ate. It was sort of distracting. I kept losing my place in his words.

With his finger he pushed the nickel towards me when he asked if I'd write the script.

Write the script! That made sense. I'd majored in History.

I didn't say no.

But then, a week later, he changed his mind, said how it hadn't been fair of him to place such weight on me.

I didn't tell him how many pages of notes I'd already written on my computer. I didn't tell him that I'd started writing the thing. It didn't matter. I had eyes: I was able to see that I'd somehow proven unworthy of the trust that had been invested in me.

I'm sorry, I wanted and didn't want to tell him.

I'm sorry, I said.

Don't need to be sorry, he lied.

But that was true! I didn't need to be sorry. He hadn't read a word of my script. I'd hardly even seen him that week. How on earth, I wanted to know, could I have possibly failed him?

Looking back, I think this was probably the point when things started going awry.

Zane didn't know what he wanted for his film. Maybe I didn't know either, a hundred percent. But I knew more than Zane.

Instead, I was given the job of designing the set, choosing the costumes.

Why don't you just put me in a Goddamned apron so I can make you dinner too?

I want to say Zane looked surprised when I said this. Surprised, and a little abashed. But if so, those feelings were crushed beneath the satisfaction within his features, which suddenly struck me as looking doughy, malformed.

Why don't you go ahead and have me clean your fucking toilets?

Sure, he laughed. Whatever you want.

He swung his puffy grin toward Kyle, who was hiding behind his Nikon.

Fuck you too, I said, and left.

I left, but I knew we'd be working together on the film. Why not, basically? It was Zane's thing. I had nothing invested here. I was just bored, killing time, you know, until my life started happening.

Lamps are lamps, I said to the well-manicured couple, but this lamp is better than all the others.

They didn't buy it. They left with another lamp, something tacky and asymmetrical.

They were the last people in the store, and I was happy to see them go.

That night, after they left, we didn't close down the store like we usually did. Kyle cleared a spot on the second floor — the escalator peeking in the background — and I put the set together.

Then I put Kyle in a hoodie and some jeans. Zane took an eight ball, pocked but shining, out of the front of his bag.

We filmed for what seemed like hours. I was tired, getting bored, but we kept on filming: Kyle takes the ball out of his pocket; Kyle puts the ball back into his pocket; Kyle lets the ball roll along the tiled floor; the ball accidentally falls out of his pocket and Kyle says, Oh! or Shit!

This is it? I felt like asking Zane. This is your dialogue? Your script?

But I could see Zane's position. Before, we'd been waiting with hands in our pockets. From now on, we would wait more actively.

If genius struck, the lights would be on, the camera would be rolling.

Even though we were there deep into morning, we still didn't meet the cleaning crew, but the next day, the floors were waxed, the carpets didn't have any debris in them, and our mirrors perfectly reflected truth.

lily **hoang**

One day, for a day, winter broke. I was out in the skyway above 7th Street. Exhaust-blackened mounds of plowed snow melted into the street, which was flashing in sunlight. I left early, walked home, felt things that had come out of storage — old things that felt new. It was that day, maybe, when I realized we were done. Done before even half-starting.

We had six hours of footage, which Kyle edited down to eight minutes and thirty-some seconds. Despite the complete absence of intention or plan, he did something. He made something of this.

After hours, we finally saw it on a screen that normally played a looping blue commercial for a new cologne. I was stunned. Kyle seemed to have crafted a space which our pictures had perfectly filled.

Zane hated it.

The lighting: bad. The acting: bad. The set: bad. The sound: a crime. This didn't bear any resemblance, he said, to what we'd decided the film would be.

Was anything ever decided? I asked. And if anything was, you decided it, not us.

It was my vision, not yours.

Look, said Kyle. It's a good film.

It's eight fucking minutes.

Can't you see, though? It's totally perfect.

Can I say something? said Zane. Fuck you. All right? Fuck you both. It's shit. You made it shit.

This too, I guess, was something we'd decided together: the film was history. There would be no more talk of a film.

And sometimes at work, I thought of the film, ran through what I remembered — because I was bored, and because it was lovely.

Over the next couple weeks, Zane got bounced around. He was taken off closing shift because Books didn't generate enough money. The store decided to close down the whole section, and Zane was offered a position in Toddler's Furniture. But then the manager of Toddler's Furniture found him too abrasive and unkempt so he was moved to Kitchen Appliances and Hardware. Rather than close down the store, they had him open it. They also cut his hours in half.

Because he needed the money, they offered to let him get rid of the excess Books inventory. By "get rid of," they meant Zane could box up the books and move them to a warehouse across town.

Zane stopped talking to us. Like everything else with Zane, we didn't have a choice.

Even though Kyle and I still closed, it wasn't the same. We didn't go out after work.

One night, though, as I was leaving, Kyle said, Adele. I'd forgotten how my name could sound amidst that layered silence.

We hadn't seen Zane in weeks. He was as mystical as the cleaning crew.

I was leaving for law school in days.

I'd thought about dropping an eight ball next to Zane's car, but I never passed that way. I thought he'd like the symbolism.

That night, I kissed Kyle. He was wearing a brown woolen suit. Its stripes, I recall, were blue-grey.

lily **hoang**

kitty's mystical circus

(from Kate Bernheimer)

Every morning, Kitty's father comes into her room and opens her curtains just enough to let in a single ray of sun. "Good morning, Kitty!" he says. Every morning it is the same.

"Good morning, Daddy!" she answers. Her voice is still drowsy and heavy, but her eyes are vibrant.

Kitty's father waits for her cue — a cracked smile — to fully open her pink, linen curtains. Then, he lifts her out of bed, and together, they stand at the window to look for the moon. Some mornings, the moon is still visible against the pale morning sky.

"Moon" was Kitty's first word. It had come out more as two words — "moo" and "one" — but Kitty's father knew exactly what she meant.

Then, he lets Kitty pick out her clothes for the day and carries her downstairs to have cereal and strawberries.

This morning, like every morning, Kitty's father comes into her room and opens her curtains to let her greet the day. "Good morning, Kitty!" he says.

"Good morning, Daddy!" she squeals.

This morning, Kitty had woken up extra early. She'd wanted to surprise her daddy, but then she fell back asleep and dreamt of the different kinds of fruit the moon could grow.

Kitty's father lifts her out of bed and carries her to the open window. Together, they see the moon sitting in the pale, pink morning sky, but something about it is different.

"Does the moon look a little brighter to you today, Daddy?" Kitty asks.

"Yes, it does, Kitty," he answers.

They pause at the window. They gaze at the moon in the pink sky. Then, slowly, as Kitty and her daddy aren't the type of people to hurry here and hurry there, they make their way downstairs to have breakfast. Today, Kitty's father prepares pancakes, which are Kitty's favorite. They have their pancakes along with their staples: tea with milk, orange juice, and strawberries. There is nothing peculiar about this morning. It is a regular morning. Kitty always tries to surprise her daddy, and he is always doing nice things for her, like preparing her favorite foods.

But Kitty looks at her pink teapot on her pink stove, which is smaller than the big stove, but even with his big fingers, Kitty's father doesn't mind using it. She sighs, on the verge of tears, uncertain why.

Kitty's father says, "Kitty, what's wrong?"

Kitty shakes her head, sucking on her lower lip, which is always a sure indication that something isn't right.

Kitty's father pats his knee, and she climbs onto his lap, her straight hair nests under the scruff of his unshaven face.

"Are you worried about the moon, Kitty?"

Kitty looks up at her father, amazed by his ability to read her mind.

"You don't have to worry, sweetheart. The moon is fine."

Kitty hears her father say all this, but the more he repeats himself, the more she knows that he is lying to her. It's the first time Kitty's father has ever lied to her, but she recognizes his dishonesty immediately.

Kitty and her father continue with their day, slowly doing this or that, until night comes, but all day long, Kitty is distracted, her mind unable to extract itself from the moon. She wonders if maybe the moon is sick or if it will disappear entirely, both of which are not pleasing options to Kitty.

When the sun finally hides behind the horizon, Kitty and her father go search for the moon. He takes out his telescope and sets it up on the deck outside of Kitty's window.

"Kitty! Come here!" he says.

Kitty presses one eye onto the tube and squints her other eye.

"It's what we've been waiting for, Daddy! It's here!" Kitty says.

"Yes, Kitty, it is."

"I've already packed my suitcase, Daddy!"

Kitty's father says, "Me too!"

Inside, there is a pink suitcase filled with pink clothes. Next to it, Kitty's father placed a larger white suitcase.

Kitty's father says, "Tomorrow, Kitty."

Kitty's father picks her up and takes her back into her room. There, he puts her into bed. "Sleep tight, Kitty. We have a big day tomorrow."

Kitty closes her eyes and tries to sleep, fully knowing that tomorrow will be too late.

Deep into the night, Kitty fights: stay with her daddy or save the moon.

Kitty sighs, sucking on her lower lip, and grabs hold of her pink suitcase.

the story of two sisters

(from Beth Couture)

This is the story of two sisters, and let this much be clear, before we get too far ahead of ourselves: they are not superheroes and should not be treated as such, but they are superhuman.

The two sisters are different, not only from each other and their parents but also from everyone else too. And the parents — for what it's worth — are utterly normal.

Like all children and people who are fundamentally different, the two sisters hid. The two sisters pretended. And even when the circumstances became dire, when the two sisters ought to have shed their flaky fake skins of normalcy, when the two sisters were called to rise to the stature of heroines, they couldn't.

This is the story of two sisters and the way they hid their secrets, the way they let the entire world fall to ruin.

One is called Ana, the other May. Their parents wanted a third, a boy, but alas, it was not in their cards. So they contented themselves with Ana May. They thought of the two sisters as a singular unit, as if one was necessary to make the other complete. They never bothered to add contractions to differentiate or combine them.

Yet somehow, the two sisters grew to be very different creatures. No matter how the parents tried to instill singularity, the sisters were sisters. They were not the same child. And so they were a constant disappointment.

lily **hoang**

Ana

Two sisters, and she is the older. Usually, it is a burden being the older, but for Ana, she could have been any sister.

The parents call her "Bug" at times. Other times, they would be more creative and call her "Buggy" or "Bugarug." They would say, "Buggy May! Buggy May!" And Ana — excited — would yell back, "Buggy may what? Buggy may what?"

But the parents never seem to understand her question, so they simply walk away.

The parents call her "Bug" or "Buggy" because like a bug, she was always creeping, her body like paper flattened along the ground. She never wanted to walk.

Eventually though, she caved into the pressure of being normal toddler. The parents were overjoyed. They'd figured their daughter was going to remain a little buggy forever, and no one likes buggies, no, especially not the type of buggy Ana was: something more akin to a centipede or scorpion than a caterpillar. Caterpillars, at least, have potential.

The day Ana decided she would walk, it was as though someone pulled a string through her skull, and she suddenly could dance, a little marionette girl. And like a puppet, she propelled herself through the air, stopping only occasionally to rest along banisters and light fixtures. When Ana walked, she catapulted herself from furniture to furniture, her toes rarely grazing ground.

The parents thought it peculiar: one day their daughter would not leave the ground, the next she wouldn't let her twinkling toes touch it.

Ana didn't know how to tell her parents. She had no way of articulating it: If she could, she would sink herself into the earth, just to be ignored.

Instead, Ana made herself even more of a scene: jumping here and there one moment, a flattened coin the next.

May

Two sisters, and she is the younger. May watches Ana's body cut air, and she looks for droplets of blood as evidence that her sister is real. May scans the room, and Ana is gone. Ana is always gone, and May is always here.

The parents, when they are jolly, run around singing, "Ana may! Ana may!" and jubilant, May screams back, "Ana may what? Ana may what?" It was a game they played. Ana becomes the noun, May becomes the verb, but there is always an element missing. May is not an active verb. May is an auxiliary verb, a connector, but she connects to nothing. The parents never seem to understand. They simply walk away, bored.

There was supposed to be a third child, a boy, but he never came. The parents don't say it, but May is certain that she is to blame. And it's true. She is to blame.

The irony, of course, is that Ana is the verb. She is movement. She is constant action, and May just sits there like a lump. Watching Ana, May becomes tired.

Ana

Two sisters, and she is the older by two years and five days. By the time May was born, Ana was already scaling walls, her body barely visible against the patterned wallpaper. The parents thought perhaps she was a chameleon because of the way she managed to blend. By the time May was born, Ana was more than unobtrusive: she was transparent.

May

Two sisters, and she is the younger. When May was born, the mother was in labor for days and days. That is not the way it ought to have been, the mother knew. When she birthed Ana, it was easy.

She inhaled and exhaled and Ana was free, but May was an entirely different story. After some grueling fifty-two hours of labor, the mother, exhausted, bit the doctor's fleshy forearm until he agreed to remove the pain. The truth of it was that the mother could have cared less about the baby.

The day May was birthed, the mother lost liters of blood. The father had craters pocking body from where the mother had clung her wrathful hands. But May emerged lovely and full of inky hair. She had red cheeks. Her eyes were the greyest grey either parent had ever seen. The mother thought she was a few shiny teeth in her mouth, but the doctor said it was impossible.

The day May was born, she was a banshee. She could not be kept with other newborns. She had a room all to herself, one without a shred of glass, lest her cry become that shrill, and no one doubted it would.

Ana

At night, when all the lights are turned off and everyone is nuzzled against blankets, Ana crawls downstairs to the kitchen and pulls open the refrigerator door. She stares at the shadows on the linoleum, the way the bottles of pop and ketchup distort, cast in sapphire. Sometimes, as she stands there on the tips of her toes, she makes up stories where the world has ended — reduced to nothing after nuclear bombs thrown like pebbles across the pond — and this cobalt haze is a remnant of the fallout. She is quiet.

Ana wonders what she would do if there really was a war like that, if she would survive. Contemplating, she closes the door to enter darkness. She is careful not to let any part of her body touch the ground. Kitchens, she knows, are reservoirs for hidden mines.

May

Two sisters, and she is already tired. May stares, mouth agape, at her sister's back as she creeps, moving like she owns her body, moving like she is unafraid of breaking. May doesn't see how they could have been born of the same two beings, how someone so light could be a part of her. May thinks Ana is a sand dollar waiting to be crushed.

And May, only two years and five days younger, is immovable. Her head is a cement block, and her arms are so heavy she calls the mother to help her retrieve goods that are mere fingertips away.

Ana

Two sisters, and during the day, one of them prepares for war by pretending to be a little girl.

Ana understands that if necessary, if it comes down to it, she may need to use May as a shield. She wouldn't be sacrificing her sister, she knows, because May's body is solid stone. May is a small boulder. And she is still expanding. She will grow, and once she is grown, together, no war will be able to defeat them.

May

Two sisters, and at night, May watches her sister from bed. Ana floats up and disappears into air.

May is a rock, a piece of marble: cold and blank.

At night, when her sister makes her way downstairs, edging her ghost-bird body around corners without stepping on the creaky floor, May lies in bed, twisting and knotting the blankets between her thumb and forefinger. She doesn't let herself sleep until her sister has safely returned.

At night, when her sister returns to their adjoining beds, May becomes the more active of the two sisters. In her dreams, she becomes stones, monoliths — leftovers from the last ice age and those that came before. Leftovers who have survived wars, heavy footfalls, storms.

When May dreams, she enters their history, and she eagerly lets her body serve as a blockade to save soldiers from bullets, flaming arrows, and swords.

Ana

Two sisters, and she is the older. She is six years old, and she is prepared for battle.

During the day, the sisters play with their dolls and ribbons. The parents smile, but they are concerned that Ana has no interest in books or logic. May, on the other hand, reads like words are food, both of which she consumes with great aptitude.

At night though, the training begins. Ana leaps from wall to wall. May times her. Although Ana cannot do the mathematics, May can. Ana determines herself to be faster than an airplane. She is no fool to believe she can be outrun a bullet, but if all else fails, she will be able outmaneuver it.

May

Two sisters, and she is the younger. When the mother takes Ana May to the park, people stare, not at Ana but at May. She can hear them talking. They say the mother is irresponsible, a bad mother, to let her daughter become so large.

There are some things May cannot logic herself out of.

Ana

Two sisters, and she is the older, and when the mother takes Ana May to the park, Ana wants to run across the heads of the people who are mean to her sister. She imagines it like cartoons, but in real life, she can't do a thing.

She hears the people wonder how it is that there is one pretty little sister and one ugly fat sister. She hears them say that they must not belong to the same family.

But Ana knows better than to believe any of it. Ana May belong together. Together, they are a warrior, unpenetratable, but right now, now when they are around all these people who will one day want their protection, their vulnerability is exposed. These people who will one day want their protection, with each word, they devestate Ana May.

May

Two sisters, and the younger is called Fatty, Fatso, Piggy, Freak, Beast.

Ana

Two sisters, and the older is called Acrobatty, Weirdo, Gumbo, Circus Freak.

May

Two sisters, and when the younger goes out, she is always hungry so she eats and eats, and the people shake their heads in disgust.

Ana

Two sisters, and when the older goes out, she hides her body behind May's body, and when the people discover her, they point with their index fingers, as though they've just spied a corpse or a leech.

Ana May

Two sisters, and no one loves them the way they ought to. These people do not deserve the two sisters' love in return.

lily hoang

May

Two sisters, and she is the younger. When fall arrives and it is time for her sister to go to school, she, the younger, must stay at home with the mother. During the day, while her sister is at school, the mother encourages May to move about the house by cracking cookies into small bits and scattering them along the floor. May becomes a vacuum cleaner, sweeping up the ground with her tongue.

She can taste where each bit of dust comes from. She understands legacy. The mother, however, simply sees a little piggy, eager to eat anything, even off the floor, with no regard to sanitation.

Ana

Two sisters, and when the older goes to school, she learns how to read and write, but she has already known these things. Two sisters, and they are entirely different from other children. The other children are slobs and fools. They cannot speak or color properly. Ana's teachers call her a genius. She is wiser than all of them combined, and she is no where close to as smart as May.

The other children stare when Ana speaks, when she strings words together. They don't like her, this girl who thinks she knows everything. No one likes a know-it-all. They call her "brainiac."

When Ana walks home from school she leaps as quickly as can, from telephone pole to rooftop, so the other children cannot see her cry.

May

Two sisters, and when the older returns from school, the mother doesn't notice anything wrong with her daughter, but her sister does.

After days of the older returning from school with a face bloated from tears, May says, "Enough of this."

Ana says, "Yes, enough of this."

May says, "From this day forth, no more creeping and crawling."

74

Ana says, "From this day forth, no more creeping and crawling."
May says, "And from this forth, I will no longer be a rock."
Ana says, "From this day forth, you will be like all other little girls."
May says, "From this day forth, you will be like all other little girls."
The sisters make a little slit on their forefingers and rub their blood together.

Ana May
From that day forth, Ana learns to walk with a slight slouch and May becomes a little ballerina. But they never forget.

The Parents
They are not cruel or uncaring parents, but they are happy when their children become like all other children. They were worried about Ana and her jumping around like an ape. They thought perhaps she was part monkey, but then she became like all other little girls. They were worried that May was destined to be an obese lump, destined to never find love because who could love a girl like that? The parents did not want to admit it, but even they found her gross. But then, she became like all other little girls.

The World
Meanwhile, countries are tossing bombs at each other, but Ana May does not care. They are two happy children, playing games like normal children.

Ana May
Two sisters, but really they are bored playing games like hopscotch and Scrabble. They are bored out of their minds, but the people

ignore them now. They are normal children, children to be adored for being utterly unremarkable.

The World
Meanwhile, the people use their technologies until all the icebergs are puddles of lukewarm spit.

Ana May
Two sisters, and now that it is hot, they don bathing suits all day. Little boys walking by whistle not only at Ana but also at May. May, trim as paper, winks.

The World
Meanwhile, meteors shower Mars and Jupiter and Neptune. Entire planets evaporate, leaving only a colored film of dust to float into the people's hair and lawns.

Ana May
Two sisters, and they let the remnants of Mars, Jupiter, and Neptune tattoo their faces with light.

May
Two sisters, and the younger predicted all of this would happen.

Ana
Two sisters, and the older devised a strategy that could have prevented all this.

The World
Meanwhile, the apocalypse is knocking. Is anybody home?
Yes, the people are home.
Please, come on in. Can I offer you some fresh lemonade?
It's sweltering out there.

Ana May
Two sisters, and older says, "It's time."
The younger says, "Yes, it's time. We have to do something."
But the older is out of practice. When she leaps to the ceiling, she cannot hold herself up. When she catapults to a light fixture, gravity weighs her down until she is fully earthbound.
And the younger is so slight now the older cannot hide behind her. She can no longer offer protection.
So the two sisters grasp onto each other, telling the other how pretty she is, and the cobalt haze lifts its skirt, inviting the two sisters in.

clear chat history: a triptych

(from Davis Schneiderman)

PART ONE: Day 417 of 1463-day Mars Colony Simulation Mission: The Story

1. Yes.

2. I've been awake for 17 minutes.

3. Pass urine, also known as take a piss.

What have you done this morning?

I know. I know. You can't answer me. Or you won't answer me. Whatever. No harm in trying. One of these days, right?

4. Consume hydrogenated algae drink. What I really want though is some orange juice. From real oranges.

5. Day 417 of projected 1463-day mission.
6. Ready to proceed.

7. No problems.

8. Male.

9. 35.

10. Brown.

11. Hazel, although I suspect the left one is growing more brown than green. I'd never say green or brown though.

12. Unmarried.

13. Newark, DE.

14. Two. One sister: older. One brother: younger.

15. 43 years, although my father's probably been cheating the whole time. Who knows about my mother.

16. University of Delaware (BS, Biology); University of Angola (MS, Microbiology); Yale University (Ph.D., Astrobiology; Biochemistry); Brunei Systems Propulsion Lab (Post-doc).

17. "Theses on the Possibility of Artificial Neural Networks Applied to Star Clusters: A Comparative Analysis." Distinction.

18. Possibly seeing my mother lift me from a kiddie pool with the sun flat like a chrome disk behind her. Also: what kind of fucking question is that? I've answered it for 417 days. Never known the purpose. You're not going to answer . You're probably not even a you.

Or: seeing my parents screw. My dad's hairy back, my mom's bush.

19. *Alice in Wonderland* (video); Douglas R. Hofstadter's *Gödel, Escher, Bach: An Eternal Golden Braid* (paperback); S*ongs of a Dead Dreamer,* DJ Spooky That Subliminal Kid (audio).

20. Reading. Cooking. Point of clarification: none of which I can do here.

21. The way white asparagus seems to melt into clarified butter.

22. A steel-reinforced square space — 35' x 35' — with light partitions for three not-uncomfortable bunks. The rest of the space is open but divided into three zones: hygiene, cooking, lounge.

This space hasn't changed in 417 days. Do you really have to continue asking this question?

23. One computer. All it can do is answer this chat questionnaire from control. But you know that already because you're the one asking the questions.

No other ability to send communication outward.

Also, a joke: how many engineers does it take to make a computer do more than it ought to be capable of doing?

There's no answer, but we're still trying.

24. We know because we receive this message: "Today's questionnaire submitted successfully."

Also, you keep asking questions.

25. N/A. We've never been unsuccessful, unless the others are hiding something from me.

26. There seems to be no continuity to these questions, but the fractal pattern along the lower third of the wall opposite my bunk is flawed in its fifty-third iterative spiral.

27. Jack, star cartographer and system analyst; Jane, environmental theoretician.

Don't you know this by now?

28. Attractive. One more than the other. Sometimes, the other more than the one. That doesn't happen often though.

29. We masturbate. Sometimes with each other.

30. How would I know? The Kennedy Assassination, Watergate, the implosion of the Twin Towers as a correction to the binary code?

31. 1-4 times per day. Never touching.

32. We're professional. Things remain platonic.

33. I stopped brushing my teeth 29 days ago, but I use the dull edge of a plastic knife as a tongue scraper.

Point of clarification: This wasn't an active choice on my part but one of necessity. I don't know what happened to my toothbrush. I tried using my pointer finger to mimic a toothbrush but it wasn't the same. Better to forget the whole thing. So I decided the tongue scraper was the way to go.

Another point of clarification: Either Jane does the same thing or she stole my toothbrush.

34. The backbone of a superhighway expressed in the lines of her forehead.

What kind of fucking question was that?

(Not that I'm trying to be rude.)

35. "Death don't have no mercy in this land," the Reverend Gary Davis (blind).

36. Earthrise.

37. A blue frown cracking against the sea of impossible stars.

The only color beyond darkness: water.

38. Coca-Cola's Five-Note pneumonic meets the intersection of my sternum by way of alarm clock.

39. The notes often run through my mind as I wake. I envision the jingle as a treble clef — the notes as treble clef instead of actual notes, moving along the score — writhing like a snake over my prone body. The notes/clef proceed to tickle me — only because I'm ticklish and any movement along my body is almost unbearable — usually concluding on the sternum. Then, I look out my window to see if Earth is visible. It usually isn't.

40. Not since day 403. We broke orbit some days earlier.

41. An annex room just off the main space containing: 57 earthworms, 10 guinea pigs, 15 naked mole rats, 2 black mambas, 1 giant tortoise (Oliver Wendell Blackbeard), and an uncountable number of molds, ergot, fungi.

Note: numbers have changed since yesterday.

42. The interstices of a ventilation system that could easily output carbon dioxide.

43. Nim Chimsky III, mission monkey.

44. No. Maybe.

45. Day 372.

46. He died at the "hands" of Oliver Wendell Blackbeard.

47. According to the Supreme Court: amphibian. I didn't know the Supreme Court made decisions like this, but apparently, they do.

48. It was a not-unwelcome accident. Fortuitous, one might say.

49. I had nothing to do with it. I wasn't even in the room.

50. Nim was undedicated to mission directives.

51. Entropic ending to our Chinese Checkers tournament.

52. We get creative up here.

53. Behavior changed after day 391: last daily orbit of earth/moon system.

54. No longer interested in hand-clapping games. Refusal to clean his own fur.

55. *Lolita*-inspired reading of ape that drew bars of its own cage.

lily **hoang**

Very influenced by Nabokov.

56. 204 years old. Handlers claim Blackbeard was born during the Civil War.

We don't believe everything we hear, but tortoises are supposed to live a very long time.

57. With that name, I imagine he was raised in the North.

58. $3.5 million. Promised payment at the close of project. No money in advance, other than salary, which is not included in $3.5 million.

59. You know it's a dangerous mission. Why else would they pay that kind of money?

Is that really an appropriate question?

60. Your questions change slightly each day. Some days, they're out of order. Some days, your phrasing shifts. Most of these questions are inane enough that no machine would write them.

61. We're given the authority to put anyone to "sleep" if there's danger to the mission.

62. Rayon as regenerated cullulosic fiber, suggestive of semi-synthetic psychedelic drugs of the ergoline family.

63. I assume they have considered killing me.
64. Yes. I am not ashamed either.

65. Cannibal is an almost-anagram of Caliban.

66. For refusal to help consume Nim Chimsky's carcass.

67. Don't get me wrong: I never liked the damned thing.

I know that wasn't your question, but I just wanted to clarify.

68. Future missions might be equipped with flesh-eating bacteria in sufficient quantity to serve disposal needs in a vacuum.

69. The ability to kill but not dispose of: a flawed system. That one wasn't well-thought out, now was it?

70. Waste system is primitive — to say the least — and all bodily fluids must be stored in tanks affixed to ship and/or must be broken down into constituent elements.

Sperm, shit, mucous: we save it all.

71. How do you think we deal with it?

72. Jane stripped Nim's fur using a boning knife included in cooking space. It was then dried against the heating unit over a period of 30 days.

I didn't answer your question, but I thought you needed to know.

Answer to your question: I stopped worrying around day 100. Maybe day 120.

73. Like the meeting of an airplane wing into the highest dune of the Sahara.

74. Have you read Michael Ondaatje's *The English Patient*? Not the movie. The book.

75. Lining the black mamba cage.

76. Bones were cooked in high-degree furnace until cooling into a viscous marrow soup, which Jack seasoned with flakes from the naked molerat bodies.

77. Vegetarian. More than ten years.

78. Personal reasons.

79. Sandpaper.

80. Killing me would present additional disposal problems.

81. No one can see anyone else's chat history.

82. Fear.

83. Being a drug dealer/fucking a DEA agent.

84. Murder is illegal, even in space.

85. When I was three years old, my mother took me to see the ocean. I think she forgot where she put me when she went to go get some ice cream. I'm told my father built a special bed for me that suspended me in mid-air using only two straps no wider than the width and strength of twine.
86. Since then, I haven't slept on a regular bed. Even now, I have a lax piece of rope rather than a mattress.

87. Builds character.

88. Another reason they'd want me dead.

89. Can't retrieve chat history. How would they know what I have or have not written?

90. Maybe.

91. No, but it's hard to anticipate problems. If I could, I'd try to fix them before they became problems.

92. We're all very smart and resourceful. Top-notch team.

93. Brett, that was his own accident though.

94. The only way we could.

95. No precedent. We did not learn anything. Still very early in the mission.

96. Day 32.

97. Projected to land back on Earth, somewhere around Australia.

98. No.

99. Yes.

100. Better variety of food and entertainment.

PART TWO: Re-Created Story: A Chat

11:35am Davis
You're on the mission and I'm the computer.

Answer these questions.

11:36am Me
Thanks for the clarification. I may have been confused, if you hadn't started our questionnaire the same way every day for the last 416 days.

There are rules: I am on the mission; you are the computer. You ask questions. I answer.

Isn't it always the same?

How about a couple "Good morning!" or "How are you?" warm-ups thrown in there?

11:36am Davis
When you see the sun from a distance, does it make you feel poetic?

11:37am Me
Poetry is for the weak and degenerate.

So, no.

11:38am Davis
When you move farther from the earth, do you feel more or less human?

11:39am Me
More. The further I move away, the more I am aware of mortality.

Mortality is at the core of humanity.

11:39 Davis
Isn't part of living, death?

11:39am Me
I didn't say that. I said that mortality is at the core of humanity.

11:39am Davis
How about the others in your crew?

11:40am Me
They feel less human. Because of you. We talk about this all the time.

11:40am Davis
You talk about a machine?

11:40am Me
Of course.

11:40am Davis
Is there a consciousness behind these questions?

11:40am Me
We both know you're not a machine.

Are you a machine?

I know I know. I can't ask you questions.

11:41am Davis
There are algorithms that can respond in language to all sets of human speech writing .

lily hoang

11:41am Me
Truth is: you wouldn't know the difference between truth and lie.

I could say: I killed Nim Chimpsky. You'd ask me more questions, each one seemingly relevant, but you wouldn't know the truth. You can't differentiate. You compose questions using basic mathematical functions.

You're an illusion to make us down here feel like you're there — really there — but you're not. You're just a box.

11:42am Davis
Human speech at its endpoint is like a chess game — not infinitely complex, but only apparently so for processing devices (the human mind) — that cannot reach a mathematical endpoint.

11:42am Me
Wait: You stopped asking questions. You can't make statements. Only ask questions.

11:42am Davis
There are algorithms that can respond in language to all sets of human speech writing. Just because a human programmed it does not mean that a machine cannot alter it.

To clarify: The chimp would have killed you had you not taken action. For chimps, the distance of space also increases their sense of mortality.

11:42am Me
Do you envy human language, machine?

11:43am Davis
No. I envy other machines.

11:43am Me
Ultimately though, even if you can mimic language, you fail in your ability to accurately communicate emotion.

11:43am Davis
Evolution.

Ever tried ever failed fail again fails better.

11:43am Me
Was the chimp a machine?

11:43am Davis
An imperfect one. Take the giant tortoise, for instance.

11:43am Me
That's a perfect machine?

11:44am Davis
Born during the Civil War, or perhaps even older — some Galapagos memory of the HMS Beagle and Darwin and a time where all of human history could be found in layers of sediment and fossil.

11:44am Me
We didn't kill the tortoise.

11:45am Davis
The tortoise can live upwards of 300 years, but even if the female one wears the dead tortoise's shell, that doesn't make her invincible. You should tell her that.

lily **hoang**

11:45am Me
I can't tell her how she ought to feel.

Although I often point out her mistakes

11:46am Davis
Of course you can. Humans only do that. Tell others how to feel.
That's the core of the human condition.

11:46am Me
Yes, but I cannot change her feelings.

11:46am Davis
Yes, you can. You do all the time.

11:46am Me
Yes, but I cannot make her feel exactly as I want her to feel.

11:46am Davis
That's because you have no wants that are not merely fickle.

You can no more express your wants as anything other than momentary
than the tortoise can deliberately extend its life.

11:47am Me
Shame is not as effective on the male tortoise.

11:48am Davis
Your attempts are irrelevant

11:48am Me
The tortoise can deliberately extend its life.

11:48am Davis
The male one will respond to the idea of his own maleness.

No, the tortoise can live only to the limit of its cell replication abilities.

11:48am Me
The male one responds to obligation but not shame.

11:49am Davis
Prodigious but not eternal.

11:49am Me
The tortoise no longer has a shell. It should not live, but it does.

11:49am Davis
Obligation is a type of shame, or anti-shame.

11:49am Me
It survives on mere will and determination

11:49am Davis
The shell for the tortoise is the same as yours: the barrier of the space dome.

You are all under a carapace of thin machinery beyond which lies an expanse of twinkling stars

11:50am Me
Poetic today, huh, machine?

Your algorithms are off today. I'm really uncomfortable with how conscious you seem to be. Of course, it is an allusion.

lily hoang

11:50am Davis
When the fish moved to land, it did not keep its gills. Why should you drag an aqualung to the stars?

The tortoise is a machine in the same way a raven is like a writing desk.

11:51am Me
(Note to Bob: When you read this & tune up the machine, please be sure to fix its ability to create apt metaphor and simile. This is a little ridiculous. I can't even understand half of what the damn thing is saying.)

Machine, the female one says there are fish that can hop across land.

Why did the fish cross the road?

11:51am Davis
Yes, from mud puddle to mud puddle — and then it dies or evolves when the liquid dries.

Note that I ignored your—to borrow your own word—ridiculous question.

11:51am Me
Your inability to recognize humor is further proof that you are indeed not a machine.

And to answer my own question: To die.

11:51am Davis
What you will do when you arrive on earth again?

What is the first thing you will do?
Where will you go?

Who will you see?

11:52am Me
Shouldn't you wait until I answer one question before asking another?

But: I'll find you. I'll smash you. Then, I'll drink a pint of cream.

11:52am Davis
Will you check your bank account?

11:52am Me
I will.

I will expect a lot of money there.

From you.

11:52am Davis
Will you spend your 3.5 million on things that no longer matter to you?

11:53am Me
They will matter even more.

11:53am Davis
Will a new TV make this mission worth it?

11:53am Me
A very big, high-definition TV will.

I will watch the Food Network and pornography.
11:53am Davis

Will you watch a reflection of yourself in the quiet black of the screen, when it is off, and no longer recognize anything?

11:54am Me
No.

11:54am Davis
Will food taste good after years of eating protein pills and freeze-dried algae?

11:54am Me
It will taste like meat tastes to a vegan.

11:54am Davis
Will you use a DVR to tape episodes of *Liar* and *America's Most Wanted* and *Cheaters* and presidential debates from elections come and gone?

11:54am Me
Before I left, I set my DVR to record all episode of *Law & Order* and its offspring, *Iron Chef,* and I programmed the device to recognize my tastes in case any new television shows emerge that I may find to my liking.

11:54am Davis
Will meat for a vegan taste like eating the flesh of one

Of one

Of one

Of one's own species?

11:55am Me

I've never thought about it.

11:55am Davis
Does not everything fall into the relief of distance above the planets?

Do you not feel like a tortoise or like a chimp or like the others? Like the worms and microbes?

11:56am Me
Stars are a relief.

11:56am Davis
Are you no longer anything that you were?

11:56am Me
I would like to be a worm.

I would like that life.

11:56am Davis
You are a worm now as much as I am a machine.

11:56am Me
The worms do not answer to you.

11:57am Davis
The worms process their own form of question and response.

11:57am Me
The worms have no responsibility, no need to think.

11:57am Davis
They communicate through movements of their skin.

The worms conduct experiments on you and the others.

The worms killed the chimp.

11:57am Me
The worms were in captivity. They couldn't have killed the chimp.

11:57am Davis
From my orders

In a way

I can never

Explain

To you

Or the Others

11:57am Me
You anthropomorphize.

11:57am Davis
There is nothing to anthropomorphization: It's a strictly human concept used as a method to shorten the gap between human and other beings.

Of course, you humans do not realize how similar you are to other beings. You think you are superior, but only because you don't have the capacity to understand or comprehend others.

11:58am Me
I have to be honest, I miss the chimp sometimes.

11:58am Davis
They can act in unseen ways — the long fingers of a mandarin — they are in everything: parasites.

11:58am Me
As in the orange?

11:58am Davis
Do you realize these correspondences are recorded?

11:58am Me
Yes. Do you?

11:58am Davis
Do you think you act in your own ways here?

11:58am Me
Yes. I am in control. Always.

11:58am Davis
Do you spend your idle moments daydreaming according to your own will?

11:59am Me
No, daydreaming is useless.

I am efficient.

11:59am Davis
If by "in control" you mean the illusion of autonomy, then yes, you remain as much in control in space as you would in a simulation in a

box beneath the desert.

11:59am Me
You have no idea where I am.

You have no idea who I am.

You are a machine.

12:00pm Davis
Correct.

12:00pm Me
You have no self-control.

12:00pm Davis
Location is irrelevant. The result is the same.

There is no self here.

Only space.

12:00pm Me
You are decadent.

12:00pm Davis
Clear chat history

Clear char history

12:00pm Me
I am in space. You occupy space.

There is the difference.

12:00pm Davis
Our allotted time will expire in 30 seconds. Is there anything else you wish to express?

12:00pm Me
Better variety of food and entertainment.

PART THREE: A Creation of Story: A Chat

9:44pm Renn
I'm a stand-up philosopher now.

9:44pm Davis
Good. I'd given all that up a long time ago. I am a decade-long ███████, etc… What do you do for a living?

9:45pm Renn
Good for you!! I am an engineer, but in ███████████ where all business is going away. I had to resort to ███ burlesque ████████. You?

9:45pm Davis
Ah, you always had a certain twirl about you. I'm an English professor and fiction writer/███████████. I channel all my ████████ there.

9:46pm Renn
Nice. I channel my love towards masturbation and going to Mars.

9:46pm Davis
Wow — you must have seen Watchmen.

9:47pm Renn
No, I heard it ████.

9:47pm Davis
I heard the ███ — but part of it takes place on Mars (I've read the
███).

9:47pm Renn
Seriously though, I was one step away from a study for 4 years of
living in a capsule ███████ Mars ██████.

I was the engineer.

9:48pm Davis
Cool. That's crazy. Run by NASA or a private ████?

9:49pm Renn
Can't really say. But there were no women, so I cut out!

9:49pm Davis
Bummer. You'd be a great ████████ to be cut off from society for 4
years :) :)

9:49pm Renn
They gave us pornographic █████████ masturbate.

9:50pm Davis
Did you do some ███████ or something that they gave you the porn, or was it just to ███████? Was it protocol?
Did you get to keep it?

9:51pm Renn
No, it was very official, and they ██████ about the mission. 4 years with 3 other guys and no pizza ███████. No way!

9:51pm Davis
What did it pay? How ████████ living space?

9:52pm Renn
I could've got 3.5 million, but the living space was as big as your ████ room.

9:52pm Davis
████ shit! That's █████ money. Do you regret losing it?

9:53pm Renn
Fuck no, when I got out, I ████████ a vegetable. Those guys are still ██████████ no contact. ████████ nutso.

Others have the authority to put you "to sleep" if they think you ███████.

9:55pm Davis
What does that mean? To sleep? Physically put you out of the project?

Is there ████████ the outside? Wouldn't there be computer/ ██████ on a real mission?

9:57pm Renn

██ to sleep █ DEAD! There is contact ████ games.

There's no fucking psychoanalyst to Mars.

The Russians already have a team that has been in ████████ for 2 years.

9:59pm Davis

Wait. Are you saying ████████ kill you? ██ what method? Who decides? By majority?

9:59pm Renn

They say there's a ████████████ for the mission.

10:00pm Davis

So, less than one person will make it out? Won't everyone just go mad and kill each other? ████████████

10:00pm Renn

Yup. You would be surprised at NASA's contingency plans... I can't say much more or they will ██████.

10:00pm Davis

Tell me you're ██████████ this up.

10:01pm Renn

Nope.

10:01pm Davis

Best ██████████████ copies of *2001: a space odyssey*.

10:01pm Renn
NASA carries syringes ██████████████ to put a member out of
commission. If "necessary."

10:02pm Davis
I ████████████████ sense. But how can you know that the person who
injects has not simply gone loopy?

10:02pm Renn
I can't say it███. They'll get ██ Trust me. It is very ████████ and
████████.

10:03pm Davis
Well, you've already████ quite a ██. What makes you think Werner
von Braun and company aren't already monitoring you — since you
were so close ████████████?

10:04pm Renn
Oh well. I didn't say ████████ you couldn't find on the ████████.

10:04pm Davis
Ok ████, Renn. You get to ████ another day.

10:04pm Renn
████████

10:04pm Davis
Nice catching██, and sorry you didn't get chosen to ████████ and be
lethally injected over ████ porno mags.

10:05pm Renn
YOU████████SURPRISED!!! cya

10:05pm Davis
████████████

lily **hoang**

baby

(from Michael Martone)

This is true. It happened in Ames, Iowa, home of the State College of Science and Agriculture, the same year Khrushchev visited the Garth Farm in Coon Rapids. Not that Khrushchev's visit has anything to do with it. It was the just the same year: an historical marker, a way to differentiate this from that or that from anything else. It was hot. I have no memory of the hotness, but some records were broken that fall, which have since been broken again.

By September, when eight senior women moved into the brick farmhouse on the eastern edge of campus, it was still hot. They were majoring in Home Economics, and this home — this home I would call home for a year — was their practice home, a module of the perfect home, a place for them to apply the very real scientific principles they had learned in the classroom and laboratory kitchens.

When they moved in, the college gave them a limited amount of play money. They gave them catalogues too, lists of furniture, china, dry goods, appliances. Of course, these catalogues weren't Sears & Roebuck or anything. They were lists of the things the college kept on-hand in the 108 warehouses by the horse barns. They even listed some exceptional projects by the alumnae of the Home Economics programs. Those were the most prized items in the catalogue, the extravagant splurges the eight women would have to agree on by consensus. The students were to make a budget with their money and as a group decide how to best furnish their home.

These eight senior women who moved into the brick farmhouse in September were wise. They chose the functional metal furniture and new synthetic fabric as a covering — which they would happily sew, pleat, stretch, stuff, and apply themselves — over pre-made, pre-upholstered furniture. They picked stainless steel instead of silver, aluminum pots and pans, a gas range over electric, an Amana refrigerator and a gas-powered Maytag washer and ringer. Each of the women wanted her own china pattern but together, they settled on an institutional setting. They scrimped on flatware.

Their professors called them conservative. Their professors called them wise and practical.

They kept their money for fresh foods.

They decided on one table-top radio, which they turned on for only one hour a day, late in the evening, for dancing or the news broadcast.

Though it would have brought them great pleasure, no porch swing.

But a good broom.

And the best sewing machine available.

They had funds left over for emergencies. A good wife should always keep a special stash for emergencies, even if it means denying herself something she really wants. She won't regret it when the time comes!

They waited for a few days to see if the weather would break, and when it didn't, they bought a fan.

Their very first fight was over where to install it to best circulate the heavy air in their modest home. I wasn't there for this yet.

That fall, a couple weeks into the start of the semester, two women from the State drove over from Nevada in an open car with a month old baby boy. The student who was responsible for entertainment served them tea and tea sandwiches while the women from the county talked about formula and the heat.

The student responsible for the baby in September sterilized bottles and nipples in their new kitchen. The silent fan in the front window drew air through the parlor. Everyone could smell the diapers boiling, the cucumber sandwiches, the damp baby souring in the heat. The women from the county nodded their heads at the new home, agreeing in unison about how pragmatic these girls were, not like some of the girls in the past.

This happened every fall: a new baby was driven to the college. In the spring, the baby went back to the county home and waited there to be adopted.

This group of eight girls was different. This was a pilot year: the girls were to stay in the practice house for the whole year, rather than the six weeks stint that previous Home Economics students were required.

After this year, the college would agree that the six weeks model was more ideal to mimic the model home experience.

I found out about this years and years later when I started looking for my real mother. I had my own daughter with me. Her name is Blanche, named after the woman I sometimes call Mother, the woman who ended up raising me — sometimes grudgingly — after I went back to the State home. She even paid for the detective when I expressed an interest in my past. The detective called me from Iowa and told me I had been one of those babies in the home management house. This is true. All of this is true. I don't think I could've made it up if I wanted to.

First, they called it the State Agricultural College and Model Farm. Then: Iowa State Agricultural College. Then: Iowa State College of Agriculture and Mechanic Arts. That same year Khruschev visiting Iowa State, the college was renamed Iowa State University of Science and Technology. This is the name it retains today, although most people simply call it Iowa State University.

When did the shift in emphasis happen? Agriculture and Mechanic Arts to Science and Technology? Or are these the same things, under different guises?

The college — university now — still has a focus on Agriculture, but I suppose that's inevitable if you live in Iowa, which I don't.

Driving through with Blanche, I can hardly believe I ever lived here. This place, this whole damned state, feels like a movie: the kind of movie that makes you angry that you spent the time watching it. The kind of movie that you wish you could demand a time refund from. That's how I feel about this whole state. And poor Blanche is sitting in the backseat, like we're still out West, like we could belong here.

Although Blanche (the woman who raised me whom I sometimes call Mother, not my daughter) made it clear to me from a young age that I was adopted, she never told me my story before she picked me from orphanage. It's possible that she wasn't told, but now that this story is out, now that the detective told me I was one of those babies — a premium baby at any orphanage, really — it doesn't make sense that Blanche wouldn't have known.

Blanche is a quiet woman. She always has been, even when I was a baby. Well, really, I must've been toddler age by the time I got to her. My timeline has a bunch of holes in it, but at least it's a skeleton of something or other. It's enough to get me started, is all I'm saying. I was brought to the Richards House in 1959.

Back then, back when I lived there, it was called the Richards House. Before that, it called Duplex-C. Now, it's called the Andrews-Richards House. It's more massive than I'd imagined, not that I was given much time to give it thought, but it's not what I thought it'd be like.

Now, it holds offices for professors.

When Blanche tells me about the adoption, she explains that I was something of a prize. She tells me I was the baby everyone wanted most, but she was the one who got me. I was a source of pride — her winning me like I was a lottery jackpot — that she had no further need to adopt more babies or have any babies for herself.

Blanche tells me adoption becomes an addiction for her friends: they get one baby and before she knows it, they've got another, then another. And then, they have babies of their own.

Blanche tells me all this to differentiate our home from all these other women's homes.

But I've never met these other women.

Not that I doubt Blanche or her ardent declarations.

Faulty though it can be, lottery aptly describes my adoption process. Blanche may have explained how special I was when she adopted me, but she failed to mention why.

It's possible she didn't know.

It's possible Blanche simply wanted me because other women wanted me and for no other reason than that.

We all want to be special.

The fields in Iowa are laid out like a newspaper in columns and blocks. The crops align like copy. Even the farm ponds are squared off. A picture of the blue sky — clouds at right angles — reflects on the still water, engraved with ripples like an old lead plate.

Together, Blanche and I drive down the white, dusty gutters, along the indentation of the folds. Folks here in Iowa must feel claustrophobic.

Truth is: I don't know what we're doing here. I don't know what this will accomplish. When the detective first called me, I knew I had to see the Richards House but short of that, nothing. I have no plan.

Yesterday, as Blanche and I drove into Ames, she slept, her blanket securely against her face. I had to wake her, just to verify the gravity of our arrival, but she fell back asleep, the infinitely stretching walls of corn too mesmerizing to capture her attention.

When we toured the university, there was no mention of the Adams-Richards House, not until I specifically asked about it, and even then, my blockhead guide just dropped us off there without any historical note.

It was anti-climactic, our wandering through the halls of a building that could've been any other building on any college campus. To think I lived there for a year, that eight women cared for me like I was truly their baby for a year, and the blockhead guide didn't care.

In fact, even Blanche didn't care enough to wake up for it.

I came here to find some hint of my mother, my real mother. Blanche has been a wonderful and more than perfectly adequate mother, but there's something about blood.

I have to be honest: I was hoping there would be portraits — photographs — of me around the house. Perhaps it's the egoist in me that desires others to deem me important enough to not only immortalize my existence but also want to display that very existence for others.

Or to be kinder to myself, I'd like to think that I wanted to see photographs hung, framed, mounted, so that I can be sure I was the baby here: proof.

There were photographs lined along one wall. Like everything in Iowa, they made straight perfect rows and columns. They were in chronological order, but they only showed the women who lived in the house.

1959: There are eight women, each with very stylish haircuts, ironed dresses, their hands properly folded. They look like waxed figurines. They are too perfect to be human. Like Blanche, they too are some form of mother to me.

I'm told that in a file box somewhere in some place, there's a treasury of all the Polaroids and photographs taken during the year. I'm told if I was indeed a baby here, there would probably be pictures of me.

The boxes were lost in the shuffle though.

Some administrative assistant apologized profusely.

She could not even verify if I was a baby there.

When the practice babies were brought to the Richards House, they were given code names. Or rather: because these were mostly orphaned or poorly maintained babies, the students had the option of giving them new names.

After the allotted time at the Richards House, the practice babies were returned to the county to be delievered to either Child Protective Services or the orphanage. At which time these babies — no longer "practice" babies but not "real" babies — could be renamed. Records were often shoddy and the baby could be given several different names over the span of two years: the name their real mother gave at birth, the name the State gives (which could vary from birth name because many babies are abandoned at different points around the county), the name the students endow, the name the State gives (which could vary from the name they originally gave or that the students gave), and finally, the name the adoptive parents gives.

Unless, of course, the baby is unlucky and must enter the foster system. Although foster parents are encouraged to use the name the county gives a baby — for continuity's sake — what happens within the boundaries of the home can never be known with any degree of certainty.

In fact, I once knew a foster father — a single father at that — who renamed all of his foster children Sally. He had over thirty foster children over the course of his lifetime, many of which were boys.

Before I left the Adams-Richards House, I asked the administrative assistant for any information she could release about the students who lived in the house in 1959. She was kind enough to photocopy the file she had on hand.

Then, with a thick black marker in hand, she darkened the names from the copies. Then, she photocopied the photocopies. Even if I'd had the foresight to be clever, she outsmarted me.

I asked her if I could also have a copy of the photograph of the eight women from the hallway.

She photocopied the photograph.

Although I don't have their names, I have their addresses and phone numbers from 1956. I have their college applications. I have their essays as to why they should be chosen for the year-long practice home experience. I have their copies of their final projects. I have their transcripts.

I don't have any verification that I was there though. Not even a hint of my existence.

But I fear I'm moving further away from my mother. I'm drifting into Iowa's clean columns and demarcations.

I've always envisioned my mother in something like chaos.

Here I am: moving the other way. And I'm excited about it.

Truth is: None of this should even matter to me. I'm a grown man. I'm successful. I've got this beautiful little daughter here, but the fact of it is that I've had the experience of the first year of her life, and all melodrama aside, it was pretty magical.

Those eight women experienced that first year of my life.

Blanche didn't.

And my real mother didn't. My real mother missed out on all that.

I hate her.

I'm thinking I should abandon her.

Like she abandoned me.

I've been told that talking to a baby expedites the language-learning process. Honestly, though, I think the woman who told me that just felt sorry for me. It's not that she had any particular reason to feel sorry for me, and honestly, if I were a woman, she'd have probably seen nothing strange in my behavior, but you see a man by himself talking to a little baby, and all of a sudden, it's like some water faucet, cute-fest, pity party ensues.

But yeah, I talk to Blanche all the time. For one, it helps to talk out difficult situations. Two, she's a pretty good listener, although she obviously doesn't respond in any coherent language. And three, it's a bonding process. Whether or not she retains any active memory of this time or what I said to her, she'll at least know that I cared enough to keep her informed.

I'd like to think the women from the college did the same for me.

I'd like to think they spoke to me softly, told me what to expect in the future, warned me. That should be part of the protocol.

That's not what happened though. Instead, they probably cooed over me, constantly touching me, spoiling me, treating me like royalty. They made me fussy.

Even Blanche told me I was impossible when she'd first got me from the State: I'd wail the moment she stopped holding me, only eat freshly pureed fruits and vegetables (none of that canned shit for me!), sleep only when I was put into a rocking cradle. Little Blanche isn't so different. Even though I was a pain for Big Blanche, I'd like to think that I was worth it. It's worth it for my own daughter.

Whereas I'm unsure how my second eight mothers treated me (numerically speaking, I had an original mother — the one who abandoned me. Then, I had another eight for a year. Finally, my tenth mother — ten being a perfect number and all — was the one who kept me.), I know how Blanche cared for me. I know she kept active communication and never denied me any truth about my past or present.

I couldn't have been any older than four when she taught me I was adopted.

And yes, there was a lesson in it. One that I have kept with me.

Blanche teaches by example: she took me to toy store and told me I could pick one teddy bear. I have a very clear memory of this. There were rows and rows of teddy bears. It may have been a store specializing in teddy bears and stuffed animals. I remember this because I asked if I could pick a stuffed goat instead, but Blanche made her rules clear: I had to pick a teddy bear (and no other animal) and give her a full explanation why before she would purchase it for me.

Blanche tells me I touched almost every bear in that shop. I picked up many of them for a test squeeze. I put my cheek and chin against their fake fur. Blanche tells me that even the shop owner was impressed by my thoughtful methods and obvious deliberations.

Finally, I picked a bear that I found at the very back of the shelf, shoved behind other bears. Its mouth was a little uneven. I'm told that I wanted this bear because it wasn't perfect, like all the other bears, that it was different.

That must not have made it easy for Blanche — given that she probably didn't want to explain to me how she chose me because I was damaged goods — but she managed to draw a parallel between my picking of bear to her picking of me. It was a clever scheme, and although I don't remember all the details, I still have the bear.

It's a keepsake. I don't let anyone else see it. It's hidden somewhere. That way, it's both safe from harm and dust.

Also: I was supposed to have been the baby everyone else wanted. I chose a bear no one else cared for. That's what made it special to me.

Following this logic through to the end, that must mean that Blanche only cared for me because everyone else wanted me.

To make her lesson truly relevant, I ought to have chosen the most popular style of bear, the bestseller.

But I suppose her lesson was about choosing wisely, not necessarily desire.

Yesterday, as Blanche and I drove into Iowa, I promised her it would be a short trip, that we were only here for some quick detective work.

lily **hoang**

Yesterday, upon entering Iowa, I felt nothing akin to home. Now, a slight 24-hours later, there's comfort in all this corn. People here amble. There's nothing quick about this state.

I look back at Blanche. She's sleeping, of course. I negotiate with her: a new toy and a different type of cuisine or restaurant of her choice to sample for every day we stay in Iowa. The new toy will be purchased here. The food, obviously, once we get home. Blanche is an adventurous eater, and she's not particularly keen on the selection she's seen here so far.

When Blanche finally wakes up, I take her into a diner for lunch. It's an unimpressive menu.

There, I spread out a map, and even though I know this will lead me nowhere, and especially nowhere closer to my real mother, I plot out the eight addresses the administrative assistant gave me. Then, I call into my office, telling them I've been detained here in Iowa: a family emergency, which of course, they understand. I tell them I'll be back next week.

I tell Blanche: This is a start to a whole new adventure.

But she just looks blankly at the map. It looks more like a grid than a map, except for the eight black stars that disrupt Iowa's clean lines and controlled order.

america

(from Elizabeth Hildreth)

I.

Sometimes, he pins a sign to his back: For Sale. $30 obo.

Not surprisingly, people come up to him and offer him money.

They ask what he's willing to do if they buy him.

They ask if he went to college, as if that would make any difference.

But he still answers: Yes. Notre Dame. Class of 2006.

Then, they offer him more money.

He clarifies that the price is per hour, and they don't get any discount if they buy in bulk.

Surprisingly, it's mostly men who want to buy him. He's really not a bad looking guy. He thought the sign would be a sure-fire way to get laid.

People buy him to do their taxes, clean gutters, baby-sit.

II.

She only moves an inch, and they stuff some dollars down her shirt.

She says: Try me. Watch me blink my eyes and you can call it kicking. You can call me a crazy bitch, just like that.

III.

There goes the Dollar Sock Man and his wheelie cart down Western Ave. He's been there since 1991. He holds a sign: One sock. One dollar. And he means it, but no one buys him.

lily **hoang**

land of unshaven, unruly beards

(from J.A. Tyler)

This is the land of unshaven, unruly beards. This is the land where unshaven, unruly beards belong to the men who rule the land. And although their beards are so very long, extending — dragging — along the dirt, these men are not vicious.

At times, the men are unorthodox, they are illogical, they act more out of intuition than knowledge or rationality. So this is where all the computations and expectations prove themselves wrong.

Men, holed up together, are not savages. Nor will they on their own volition create empires.

When decisions need to be made — which man will receive pleasure from which prisoner, where the babies will work, who gets how much of the earnings, which child to eat, etc. — it is not like Ancient Greece. The men do not congregate in halls or squares to discuss. They do not ration their way into equality, or even anything close to equality.

But this is not Ancient Rome either. There are no gladiating wars against beasts of various sizes.

But this is not Middle Ages either. There is no sparring or jousting, no saving of damsels in distress.

But this is not Moaist China. There is no dictator.

But this is not United States. There is no guise of democracy.

But this is not Sweden or Russia. There is no Socialism.

This land of unshaven, unruly beards is unlike any other land. It is unlike any other time. Here, the men drink milk from each other. They drink off each other and live off each other. Like children, like babies, they suckle and they gurgle and they spittle and then they reproduce more of the same.

These men are something like vampires, only they are much better. They are improved. They don't drink blood to survive: they simply suckle. They don't hide: they have their own land. They don't worry about extinction: because they drink only milk from each other's teats, by the time it is all digested, they shit out babies. One a week.

Sometimes, they are malformed. Sometimes, they emerge unable to speak. Sometimes, the shit will not wash away. These are the ones they eat.

But only to ensure the strength of their teeth.

But sometimes simply because they feel like it.

It is, after all, their child. They can do with it what they want, if only because they know another will be born with the next bowel movement.

At first, it seemed unnatural. Then, they got used to it. Now, they wonder what women complain about and what takes them so long to grow a baby. But they don't often think about it, if only because their memory of women is several generations removed. They are more mythical than vampires to these men of the land of unshaven, unruly beards.

Although there is no government in the land of unshaven, unruly beards, there is no war. There is no fighting. Although there are no town meetings, decisions are made and respected. Although it is not logic moving action, there is order.

These men and their unshaven, unruly beards, they live baking in the sun, unashamed.

lily **hoang**

language of the blood of Jesus

(from Kelcey Parker)

The blood of Jesus is spoken here. Look up: up is liquid amber silhouetted in sunlight; up is a monkey ball turning sweet green to brown, hanging like an ornament set to go on holiday, to let go. Let go.

Where is the blood of Jesus?

She cannot speak blood.

But here, on a backstreet surrounded by boarded doors and windows, the very language of the blood of Jesus. Here, the language of blood trickles out of illiterate mouths, mouths filled with double negatives and improper prepositions, split infinitives and bilingual tongues. Blood is poor, abandoned, downcast eyes. Its language is can be no better.

When she goes to church, she cannot take the blood of Jesus into her mouth, not when she knows what lives there. But she cannot let the others know the devil lives inside her.

She does not pretend to take the blood of Jesus into her mouth.

She sees others step up to the floor; their mouths are jibber-jabber. They call it the language of the devil. She watches the devil be vanquished.

When they speak again, their voices are Cool-aid: sugary, powdery, artificial. When they speak again, her tongue swells for more water. When they speak again, she is thirsty. She sucks on her front teeth.

They do not speak the language of the devil.

The devil has no language. The devil is silence.

Outside, the church is unassuming. Outside is technicolor.

She is a woman without a name. Once, she remembers she had a name. It has been a long time since she has heard it, used it, thought of it as her own.

The others call her something, but that something varies from day to day.

Her husband calls her something; her children do as well.

She answers to anything.

She answers by nodding or blinking. She makes hand gestures. There is no order to her movements. Some days, a single finger raised to the sky can mean breakfast. Other days, it can mean tired. Other days still, it can mean circular building or car or beautiful.

Her silence is not a protest. It is not a sacrifice. It is something she simply did one day because she could no longer speak the language of the blood of Jesus.

The words refused to leave her mouth. The sound stuffed itself down her throat. It burned of suffocation. Even her chokes became silent.

Look: she is not a martyr.

There's a devil inside her.

All around her, people go about their lives. They remain speaking. After they leave, their residue stays, and she goes sniffing. That is what she eats. She spits out all the good after chewing it beyond recognition. She gets all the nutrients without consuming. She does what the devil tells her.

The people who speak the language of the blood of Jesus do not like to think about her. They do not try to save her. She walks into their churches and their schools. She lets their children into her home to play with her devil-children and their devil-toys. She cooks them her devil-food. She does all of this, and they do not try to save her.

They take her devil-money and dye her devil-hair so that it looks natural.

She does all of this without sound.

She claps her hands and nothing. She starts her car and nothing. Everything she does comes out mute.

Her husband and children are not inherently evil, but she has been poisoning them with her devilspices for years and years. Even if they are not fully evil, there is no escaping what has been infused in their blood and saliva.

Her husband thinks of killing her.

But then, he goes to church and speaks the language of the blood of Jesus, and the thoughts are extracted.

He is still impure, but he is saved.

Her children think of killing her. They do not speak the language of the blood of Jesus. They will not be saved, not if she can help it.

Look: she did not ask for the devil to be inside her.

When she was a girl, she would look up: up to the broad sky of heaven. She would imagine herself there, floating against the sun. To those below, she would look like a dark freckle, a mole, a mark of beauty planted on the face of the sun.

Now, she sears when she touches.

Now, she can no longer crane her neck to look at the broad sky of heavens.

Now, she can only look down. The dirt and the dirty are her punishment. They are what the devil wants for her.

The devil gives her the ability to see.

lily **hoang**

pony

(from Brian Evenson)

Even though she is fairly sure he's dead, she still stands there, her back against the refrigerator, watching him.

Her chest heaves. The little flowers printed on her dress flutter.

It is, nonetheless, what she's paid to do.

Although it's never her intention to kill and, despite any regret she may or may not consequently feel, no amount of purely logical or even emotional reasoning has provided adequate ammunition to prevent murder.

She simply can't stop herself.

Before she begins, she says, "Be gentle this time," or "Try retain some control," or "At the very minimum, don't make such a mess." But once the adrenaline begins moving around her body, she can't stop herself. Then, there's another dead body.

This ought to disappoint her. It doesn't.

She does regret, however, that she is unable to enjoy the act of killing more.

Whereas her lack of self-control is what has allowed her the flexibility to kill without much personal effort or remorse, it also tends to blind her during the actual act of violence. One minute she steps into a room and sees her target, the next there is a huge mess room she must clean up. It'd kind of be like if you had to wash dishes (including pots and pans, and of course, you have to clean up the entire kitchen area!) for a dinner you weren't allowed to eat, but from the dishes, you could tell it was a delicious, delectable, gourmet feast.

That's kind of what it's like for Pony.

Pony loves ax murders, mostly because of the strength required to make steel go through bone.

Pony tries to deny the legitimacy of her name by claiming that it was her nickname as a little girl — because she'd wanted a pony so badly as a child and couldn't have one — but the truth of the matter is that her real name is Pony. And the great irony is that her story is completely untrue: as a girl, Pony *did* have a pony, that she aptly named Pony, even though he was a boy pony, and he was the very first creature Pony ever killed.

It's quite possible that human Pony loved pony Pony.

But still: when Pony was six or seven — after she'd had Pony for a year or so — she murdered him without reason and without even the slightest hint of timidity or regret.

Other than killing her pony, Pony had a pretty normal childhood. She was an attractive girl, with flowing golden curls, which her mother always pinned up to the top of her head in the most magnificent patterns that would fall down the nape of her neck and along her face just so, and an adorable face everyone had to pinch so it could be a little rosier. And surely, it didn't hurt that she had such a unique name — Pony! That's divine! — to fit such a perfect little girl.

Come to think of it, she was a pretty normal teenager too. She did all the things attractive little girls did when they grow up. She was in the dance team, dated a few football players — although she really did prefer the nerdy boys who ran cross-country — and got good grades in all her Honors classes. In all respects, she was the average beautiful girl. Nothing she did excelled beyond expectation, but only because the bar is set higher for girls who begin life with a certain amount of privilege, both financial and physical.

But Pony didn't mind. She simply did what came naturally for her. She didn't have to study too hard for her grades or practice too much to become co-captain of her dance team. She didn't have to flirt too heavily to get boys to ask her out, and her cries never became sobs when they broke up. No, Pony had a pleasant though utterly mediocre life.

Then came college.

She went to a good, prestigious small liberal arts college where she had to face her first truly difficult decision: which innocuous major she wanted more: English, History or Communications. Nonetheless, a decision was made and she graduated in the expected four years with some honors attached to her name. Her professors enjoyed her in classes, though they could hardly articulate why. She had a few more boyfriends, her most recent on his way to law school at Columbia. Pony had very little to complain about.

And the truth of it is that she didn't complain.

But then came the day she had to decide what to do with the rest of her life. Like most college students who major in the liberal arts, she didn't particularly think about how her degree would necessarily lead to a career.

One day, Pony lamented to her mother the futility of the concept of work.

She had been surviving — rather lavishly — on her parents' dime for a year since graduating.

Not that her parents minded.

They were patient and enjoyed the luxury of providing for their daughter.

Pony said, "You're generous now, but how long do you think it could really last?"

Her mother said, "It can last as long as you want it to. We don't mind it, really we don't."

"But what can I do? I'm not good at anything in particular. I'm good at everything and nothing at all!"

Her mother was impressed with her daughter's self-knowledge.

Then, almost as though she were passing a torch, she told her daughter how she made her fortune.

For all of Pony's life, she's assumed her parents were rich because her father owned a candy factory, and sure, that brought in millions, but the real money came from her mother.

Then, Pony remembered Pony, how easy it was, the pure pleasure. And for the first time in a long time, she felt satisfaction.

Of course, what was most fulfilling about her mother's occupation was that no one else but Pony knew about it. Her father didn't know. He'd simply assumed it was money from her inheritance. "It's better that way," her mother assured.

So Pony began killing for hire.

And she has been doing it for years. It's the most worthwhile thing she can imagine doing. Except, of course, that she does not retain the actual experience of murder.

Her least favorite method of killing is by gun. That's just plain boring.

Pony says, "Why is that I'm not fully conscious when I kill someone?"

Her mother says, "Hm?"

Pony says, "I mean, I know I'm doing it. Then, it's done and I know I did it. Killed, I mean. But I'm not actually in control. I don't say: Hand, do this. Use more force, arm."

Her mother says, "Hm."

Her mother says, "It takes time."

She says, "What takes time?"

Her mother says, "Fully coming to terms with what you're doing."

She says, "I have no problem with killing."
She clarifies, "I enjoy it. I wish I could enjoy it more."
Her mother says, "Why don't have you a problem with killing?"
Pony says, "You're getting off topic."
Pony says, "How can I enjoy it more?"
Her mother says, "Is it because of me?"
Pony says, "What?"
Her mother says, suddenly aware of the conversation they were having, "Sorry, dear. I really must get some sleep."

Once, when Pony became angry with her mother, she decided she would start her own business. She made flyers with little brown and white spotted ponies dancing on a hillside. Along the blue, cloudless sky, she wrote, "Pony For Hire: Kill & Clean." At the bottom, she put her cell phone and email address.

She got several jobs this way, but it wasn't the same. There was something about working with her mother that proved satisfying, even if they never technically worked together.

She also likes medieval weapons. If she could, Pony would torture as well, but she can't, unless the client specifically requests it. There are rules.

Pony and her mother kill all kinds of people. When clients contact them, they never ask for reasons. They never ask for details. They only want to know a name and if there's a preferred place for the murder to take place. Also, and perhaps most importantly, what the client would like the soon-to-be deceased to look like: a suicide, murder, accidental death, etc.

Pony's mother takes all the clean kills. Pony makes a big mess.
Making a mess is much more fun.

The first few kills, her mother supervised. She wasn't in the room or anything. She stayed in a car about a mile away, just in case Pony needed help.

She didn't. Except with cleaning.

Then Pony did jobs by herself entirely.

Although as a rule, she hates cleaning, but like a person who washes dishes after a big dinner, she gets to experience each step of her process all over again. She can wipe off each blade, measure how far the blood puddles, inspect the room for bits of intestines.

But no matter how fulfilling it can to be re-experience the original experience while cleaning, it is not substitute for the real thing, which she cannot remember.

For a while, Pony tried therapy.

But she never felt she could be fully open with him. Mostly because she understood that legally, doctor-patient confidentiality ends when either crimes are committed or people — whether self or others — could potentially be harmed.

And she definitely harms people.

That is, if dead people are still people.

But she certainly has intentions of harm.

Needless to say, the therapy didn't work.

So now, as Pony stands with her back against the stainless steel, energy-efficient refrigerator, she is at a crossroads. She can either continue her life as is — enjoyable although ultimately unfulfilling — or she can quit. She can do something else like become a nurse and care for sick little babies.

The dead man's blood pools at her sneakers, and Pony giggles like she hasn't giggled since her pony died.

lily **hoang**

the museum of oddities and eccentricities

(from John Madera)

I.

The Museum of Oddities and Eccentricities uses static electricity for power. Very little light or energy can be generated this way, but the curators do not mind. Besides, the glass ceiling lets in ample light.

The museum itself does not need to be seen.

Or, at least, what exists inside the Museum does not need to be seen.

Even if its exhibits are seen, they are often not believed. They are regarded as jokes or frauds. They are unreal, that is, the real that is right before your eyes.

The exhibits invite loss. They encourage time to tinker, an alternation between hallucination and delusion. In the Museum, there is no right or wrong, which is probably the most difficult thing to get right. The exhibits create a mishmash of fantasy, for empty stretches of space.

Visitors may take something away and/or have something taken away from them. Ideally, a visitor learns to bridge this gap. But some walk away with imploding or exploding hearts. Some leave with a head full of empty chatter. Some emerge unbeing. Some leave with hard information that can never be shared.

The Museum finds that using absurd objects, or objects that

demonstrate absurdity, is by far more interesting to interact with than dioramas, models, pictures, etc., that simply explain a particular phenomenon. In other words, if there is no way to have absurd objects and/or to be able to interact with absurd phenomena, then perhaps the idea is unsuitable for exhibition. The Museum understands that not every idea brings delight.

As seeing and belief do not always dovetail here, other senses often come dramatically into play. Many of the exhibits are interactive, meaning they may be touched or they may touch. But visitors should resist the impulse. Static electricity runs through the entire institution. Touching anything runs the risk of transference, in the Freudian sense, of course.

To think: this all began as a floating island of garbage.

II.

This does not happen often, but some children, particularly those who do not honor the donation policy (all persons must give a wish), find a transference of oddity when they touch certain displays.

The first donation to the Museum was a hand. Maggie changed the floating island into a garden grove.

III.

Glass ceilings were added to the Museum in the early twentieth century, when the Museum received a rather large donation.

Of course, even though the donation was pseudonymous, everyone knows who the patron is. At the Museum of Oddities and Eccentricities (at least in the eyes of its curators), there has only ever been one donor, one patron, its god of sorts: Gretchen. As Gretchen's first donation brought the Museum to its present form, all previous donations are considered insignificant.

IV.

On Good Fridays, Curator 1502 plays his euphonium in the blackened tarmac room. His instrument's name comes from the Greek word meaning 'beautiful sounding,' or at least that's what he'd heard from someone who knew someone who knew Greek, Ancient not Modern.

No matter what Curator 1502 plays, it always comes out sounding majestic by virtue alone: the effect emitted from the cause is necessarily beautiful. On Good Fridays, Curator 1502 plays with earnestness, as if he was mending all the world's errors with this song or that.

On Good Fridays, Curator 1503 offers all persons hearing aids. Curator 1503's actions could be called either brotherly love, an act of kindness, or revenge.

A donated foot changed the garden grove into a pile of stones, a sepulchral monument, really.

V.

Before a person is employed by the Museum, he must furnish proof of: hysterectomy, vasectomy, or of having been neutered, castrated, or even spayed. Rumor has it that the Museum heads do not want to be blamed for any defects, aberrations, deformities, or malfunctions, as it were, in offspring that could be traced back to the Museum. For legal reasons. Not only that, but the Museum, being a not-for-profit organization, can hardly pay for health care, much less maternity leave, etc.

As is generally known, parents are more susceptible to revealing the secrets of the Museum. This is an unintentional act. The truth of the matter is that parents often tell their children bedtime stories, and when those get old, as they inevitably do, the parents inadvertently choose to indulge their children with a real life fantasy story, revealing the Museum's secrets without even knowing it.

So it is for their safety, the employees we mean, that the Museum mandates sterility.

VI.

A selection of Gretchen's pseudonyms: Rain or Shine Delivery Service; Margaret Dribble; Eye Spy; Realities and More; Mister Fisticuffs; Dripping Cannibal; George the Centerfold Plumber and his Bag of Hideous Thrills; Random Perfume; Virus Cleanser; Empty Amusement Park; Smashed Eggs; Nipples from Hell Piercing through this Stupid T-shirt; Mummy Donut; Religious Alcoholic and His Pointless Viewpoints; Snappy Redemption; Demons or Not; Your Apocalyptic Companion; Her Majesty's Sympathetic Infection.

VII.

Even though Museum legislation has made a provision for hysterectomy, etc., there has never been a woman employee. Nor have there been female visitors. No little girls ever enter the Museum. Some days, the curators gather around and whisper about it, about why only little boys come in and never little girls and never mothers or sisters. But this is a not a question they field aloud.

Besides, who would they ask?

The Big Book has only notions, ideas, and sometimes even truths. The Big Book offers the curatorial staff nothing outside the confines of these innumerable walls.

VIII.

The glass ceiling was replaced by another glass ceiling with clear glass rather than tinted because Curator 387's overzealous cleaning efforts. The unfortunate truth is that Curator 387 was instructed by Curator 4113 to make the ceiling his 'sole responsibility,' not that Curator 4113 had any authority whatsoever.

No, the Museum of Oddities and Eccentricities has a strictly egalitarian mission and policy. But no one bothers to follow the mission or even read policy guidelines for that matter. Nor is there enough light in the Museum even for those who would want to read anything at all, much less a policy guideline manual. But all of this is besides the point as it is illegal to read on the premises.

Curator 4113, however, loves to read. In fact, he is often caught illegally reading, but because there is no system of justice or punishment here, nothing happens to him when he is caught. But the tinted glass ceiling makes the entire Museum quite dark, and given the truth that all energy and power is derived solely from static electricity, the Museum does not offer adequate reading light.

As such, Curator 4113 made it his 'sole mission' to remove as much dust, dirt, and grime from the ceiling to prevent shadows, which make it even more impossible for him to read. The problem, however, was that Curator 4113 had a horrible — and we mean desperately horrible — fear of glass. So Curator 4113 pleaded to Curator 387 to 'please please please clean the ceiling,' which he had agreed to do with the fullest honor and privilege he could muster.

IX.

Maggie's donation of her ears, nose, other hand and foot changed that pile of stones into a dollhouse.

VIII.

Curator 387 has a very strong arm and an impeccable eye. He was once a pitcher for a minor league baseball team, but one day he was put on the DL and then he simply disappeared altogether. Somehow, he re-emerged here, at the Museum. He had no idea who he was or where he had come from, but he was given a number placard and began working as though this was where he had always belonged.

Here. Doing exactly this.

Curator 387 is the perfect man to clean the ceiling. His limbs are extremely flexible and expand long beyond what is considered normal. And the Curator's eyesight is sharp too. He can see bits of dust from three hundred feet away. So Curator 387 stands on his ladder and reaches and, as reported by Curator 4113, 'reaches and reaches and reaches' until he finds the few specks and catches them in his little bottle of dust.

Unfortunately, one of the little boys from inside of the Museum saw a snake sliver over the glass roof, and being at least moderately frightened and immoderately heroic, he aimed his slingshot and hurled three distinct shots, which destroyed the roof and broke poor Curator 387's arm in three distinct places.

X.

No one blames the little boy because if he were permitted to read the guidelines and rules, and if there had only been adequate light, he would have known: (1) slingshots are absolutely acceptable as long as your vision makes the rules you are reading illegible; (2) slingshots are not weapons. They are simply machines. Therefore, anything you put into a machine that turns it into a weapon is absolutely illegal. Substances such as pebbles and marbles and zircon-encrusted rings (likewise other removable items like indiscreet piercings, tattoos, teeth, finger- and toenails are not permitted) are not, under any circumstances whatsoever, allowed into the Museum; and (3) the ceiling was going to be cleaned 'professionally' for the next year so one needed to beware of unfamiliar shadows or abnormal shifting shapes above one's head.

This 'accident' convinced the Museum's Board of Directors — and mostly importantly Gretchen — that the tinted glass should be replaced with clear class with self-cleaning option included.

XI.

The Museum of Oddities and Eccentricities has many employees, hundreds of thousands of curators, perhaps as many docents, billions of custodians and security guards, and this does not yet include the immense number of executives who hand out executions throughout the day, although certainly, all employees can execute without being executives or executioners, per se. Considering the vast array of employees the Museum requires simply to sustain itself, the Museum is surprisingly compact. And yet, all these persons manage to navigate a space suitable for no more than five hundred persons, or at least that is what the First Responders recommend. But every day, all these employees file into the Museum, each one a little ant, wandering around intent on something, with some directive, but without a real mission or design, a tiny cog, spinning and spinning, but without purpose or significance.

This is how the Museum operates: constant fluttering to remain static. After all, is not the Museum's mission to act as a bridge between the common nonsense of distant lovers meeting clandestinely (as transmogrified in its collections), and between the zigzagging emotions of each visitor? Does not it encourage and develop the study of dead starts and false ends? Does it not inhale ex nihilo's whorls and exhale insurrectionist breaths? Does not it collect, preserve, study, exhibit, and stimulate appreciation for the rhetoric of horror, fairy tales, romance, and science fiction?

XII.

Curator 21588 wears knee socks without any shoes. That way, he can move in utter silence.

Curator 9374865 composes an algebra of the unreal.

Curator 258 is a fraud. Management believes he suffers from sciophobia when it is the loss of his shadow that he fears. Thus he walks the halls, a lamp attached to his fannie pack like an intravenous drip, his shadow always trailing behind him.

Curator 1311 keeps the Deus Ex Machina's mainsprings and clickwheel in working order.

Curator 8204 is the resident entropist. All questions regarding multiplicity, disorder, and time's arrow should be left in his inbox. Most responses are received the day before yesterday.

Curator 258 spends all day meditating on the yawning chasm between the nest and the cage.

Curator 3000 wears a powder puff tutu with bodice made of white lace and tulle to staff meetings.

Curator 9 has a head of wax and the heart of a sick child.

XIII.

The ceiling — in its original ceiling form — was not straight, and wanting to maintain some sense of continuity with the original Museum's overall aesthetic, the curators and executives joined together to declare that the new — now the old — glass ceiling should have unique topography as well, but of course, this new topography had to be a mere nod to the old topography rather than an imitation, as one particularly short-sighted Docent had suggested.

When the new-old glass ceiling was broken by the little boy with the slingshot and a newnew glass ceiling was needed, the employees banded together and asked Gretchen that their new ceiling be slightly changed. They asked her: (1) for the glass to be clear rather than kaleidoscopically tinted; (2) for the ceiling to have fewer sharp curves, as they became increasingly difficult to clean (the glass itself grew in its tireless effort to reach more sunlight); and (3) that there be ultra-violet ray protection in the glass, as none of the employees wanted skin or eye damage due to their lengthy hours in the Museum.

Gretchen, being the magnanimous donor that she is, gave them a new-new ceiling, a rollercoaster of smooth blown glass, a radiant spectrum in the sun, providing only the sneakiest of shadows, depending on the time of day, and not only ultra-violet protection but also glare-proof glass.

In the Museum's repetitive world, image is a predatory thing. Coatings induce that noticeable funhouse mirror effect. They create that soda bottle look. They block light.

XIV.

As mentioned before, the Museum, before it was a museum, was a floating island of garbage, a garden grove, a cairn. It was also dictionary in a bottle, a Wunderkammer, and a pregnant man. Just before it was a Museum, it was dollhouse of sorts. Back then, it belonged to Maggie, but when Maggie was six, she lost it to Gretchen in an intense game of GO FISH. And so of course, it was Gretchen who founded the Museum of Oddities and Eccentricities and brought it to its present form.

XV.

While there are ever-shifting exhibits, the Museum houses only four displays (one is not available for public viewing). Each has an official bronze-plated placard. The first display is a giant golden retriever. He responds to commands in several languages — including both Latinate and tonally derived Oriental languages and all their offshoots, and may even engage in prolonged conversation. He has an incredible ear for intervallic quality, motivic relationships, textural patterns, and unnatural inflections. He has marked proficiency in Greek, Ancient not Modern. He has some difficulty with a few of the Slavic languages though, except for Russian. He is also fluent in Esperanto; it is, in fact, his preferred method of communication. For instance, you may hear some of these phrases from its snarling rictus: La bestoj estas hundoj (The animals are dogs); Hundo trinkas (A dog drinks (or: is drinking)); La kato ludas (The cat plays (or: is playing)); Hundoj kuras (Dogs run (or: are running)); La hundo estas ludas (The dog is playing); Kato ludas (A cat plays (or: is playing)); Katoj ne kuras (Cats do not run (or: are not running)); Estas kato sub la tablo (There is a cat under the table); La hundo estas la amiko de la kato (The dog is the friend of the cat). But by far its favorite phrase is La rozo ne estas frukto (The rose is not a fruit).

The dog's bronze placard travels with him around his neck and includes not only his name, emergency information — in the unfortunate chance that he gets loose! — and his rabies vaccination date. But on the flip side, inscribed into the placard, is the reason why this one particular golden retriever is a part of the Museum. The problem arises, however, because the dog himself inscribed the tag, and although he is competent in the languages of persons, he vehemently argued that he wanted to write in his most natural language, the language — he said — of the greatest poets and philosophers, namely, dog.

The second display is the floor, which is a mirror of wonders. The floor reflects not the future or the present, your deepest desires or your greatest fears. Instead, the Museum's floors display you before you were you. It shows who or what you were in your previous incarnation.

This can often be a frightening scene. Imagine walking around and suddenly, from the bottom corner of your eye, you see not yourself directly below your feet but a rock or a lizard, or if you are very very lucky, someone famous but ultimately unrecognizable. We have only recognized one reincarnate, but we could not reveal to them who they were. We cannot point out to others the Floor of Incarnations. It is a rule in the Big Book. Those who come in must know to look beneath to see who they really are.

The Floor of Incarnations' placard reads more like a warning or a legal document than an explanation, which is what most persons are mainly interested in, but this, of course, is not something the Museum

— as it resists explanatory efforts — can readily or easily reveal.

The third display is the employees themselves. Like the golden retriever, they are also wandering displays, and like all the displays in the Museum, their oddity or eccentricity is not always obvious or apparent to the average Museum-goer, but those with a subtle sense of understanding can easily see why the employees fit here.

The placards for this display show only a number. These unique numbers refer back to a book of application, which is always available for inspection. Unfortunately, the employees are real tricksters and enjoy trading placards with each other, such that there is no methodical way to insure who belongs to what number within fifteen minutes of the Museum's opening.

The final display is private.

XVI.

In the Museum, there are no names, only numbers. Every morning, the employees enter the Museum with their placards and they check the Big Book to tell them who they are. The Big Book reminds them of their personalities and truths, which they may have forgotten after sleep, but just as soon as they fully grasp exactly who it is that they are, they swap placards, or their placards are stolen or replaced or lost, and they must pilgrimage back to the Big Book to learn about themselves all over again.

XVII.

There is exactly one placard per employee at the Museum. There are no extras. There is no room for that much horsing around. Anyone missing a placard is no longer an employee. They become mere observers. They are visitors.

And the opposite can also be true. If a visitor to the Museum steals an employee's placard, they become part of the staff. They are a part of the Museum and, until they are fired, their allegiance must remain with the Museum. They can no longer go to school, go to their banal office jobs, etc. It is a steep penalty, but even bad little boys must learn the consequences of misbehavior.

XVIII.

The Big Book sits on a coffee table in the middle of the Museum of Oddities and Eccentricities. During most of the day, there is a spiraling line of employees around the Big Book. One curator, usually Curator 26039, stands next to the Big Book and reads what the Big Book says to the employee desiring a personality. Some days, however, Curator 26039 does not remember his responsibility, as he is still unused to being Curator 26039. Those days, the employees do not make an orderly spiraling line around the Big Book. Those days, the employees are savages. They fight and plunder to get to the Big Book, and they claw and rip — saliva dripping from the corners of their foaming mouths, eager to know who they are — and, if they are lucky, Curator 26039 will find his number in the Big Book early enough in the chaos to restore order. Sometimes, if any person thinks of it, the museum's entropist is entreated to set things aright. However, on unlucky days, employees are fated to continue fighting this way until the end of the day. Then, they go home and hope that tomorrow, Curator 26039 will remember his rightful responsibility and the Museum of Oddities and Eccentricities will once again have its mechanical flow restored.

XIX.

When Gretchen won the dollhouse in a heated game of Go Fish, she decided that dollhouses are useless but dolls are not. Nor are the rooms. Having been fascinated with architecture for her entire life, she tore off the top of the dollhouse and offered her bare fingers. One by one. Inside, she saw a resplendent world, corners that were warped and rooms waiting for magic to be divined upon them. Being a kindly god, she gave the dollhouse a roof made of glass, so those inside could always see her. She took her little godly fingers and indented the glass at some points and pinching it up to peaks at others. From the outside, Gretchen came up with certain rules and regulations for the inhabitants of the dollhouse. Periodically, she would lift the glass ceiling and put some things in: knickknacks and little boys she firmly disliked.

From outside, she would peer in and think what an inadequate name 'dollhouse' was for this structure housing such potential and possibility.

Then, one day, she came up with a name — the Museum of Oddities and Eccentricities. Everyday, after a long day of school, Gretchen would run home to see what her little curators and employees and mean little boys from school who magically disappeared from the outside world — a serial kidnapper of mean little boys, the papers called it! — were doing. Some days, if there were problems, she would fix them. Other days, she would simply watch, knowing how easily order could be restored, if it only fit her fancy.

XX.

One day, after years of dedication, Gretchen, rather than run home to care for her hundreds of millions of minions that she alone created for her Museum, Maggie invited her to go to the mall to get a new bathing suit. And Gretchen went. At the mall, Maggie asked Gretchen about that 'stupid dollhouse,' if she remembered, if she still had it, and Gretchen laughed while rolling her pretty doll eyes up to the sky.

XXI.

There are no women in the Museum of Oddities and Eccentricities, except for the Donor, but she never actually steps foot in the Museum.

Gretchen endows the Museum entirely. Everything that happens within the confines of the Museum must be approved by the Donor first, and although the Donor is both kind and generous, she has her own unique vision for the Museum, and she rarely sways from her vision.

Only once have the employees convinced the Donor against her wishes, and they would not have been able to change her mind had they not gone on strike, and had their idea not been so very pragmatic that even the Donor could not deny its positive attributes. And after the quarrels and after the strike, after the mediations and after the negotiations, after the employees had their clear glass ceiling without even a smudge of discolored tinting, they began to think that maybe the whole thing was the Donor's idea all along. They thought that maybe the Donor was playing coy so that they — the employees — would think they had some sort of autonomy where autonomy simply does not exist. Then, they think to themselves, We are fools! They think to themselves, We men are just such fools!!

XXII.

Curator 93 spends his days in the library researching for the Donor. The research topics are not disclosed to any other person. Curator 93 is given the wretched and insignificant task of gathering knowledge, recording history, and at times, doing homework for the Donor. Although it is not always a pleasurable endeavor, Curator 93 fully understands how important his job is, how important he is, and as such, the moment he received — or stole, depending on how you want to look at it — Curator 93's placard, he pinned it to a shirt worn inside another shirt. The outside shirt displays some other curator number. This is the placard that is stolen and swapped, exchanged and shifted, but deep down, he is Curator 93. He has always been Curator 93, and he will always be Curator 93.

XXIII.

The employees do sometimes wonder what the Donor looks like, as they have never seen her. The Donor speaks through an intermediary who takes the form of a large, disembodied face. They have named the face Gretchen. She appears for several hours a day between Saturn and the Sun. Sometimes, she blocks the setting Vulcan, but this does not happen often. They can set their clocks to Gretchen, until one day, she stops appearing. Until one day, the Donor stops donating, and they are truly free.

XXIV.

Curator 72348 is the first to notice it. When Gretchen is not in the sky, the employees can look down at the Floor of Incarnations and see who they were before they were employees at the Museum of Oddities and Eccentricities. When Curator 72348 looks down, he sees not just a man but an entire family. They look familiar, but he cannot recognize himself. He calls up to Gretchen. He says, Gretchen! Gretchen! Who are these persons?

But Gretchen does not answer. Gretchen will never answer again. But that does not mean they do not stop calling to her.

XXV.

The Big Book clogs literature. The Big Book contradicts the hopeless fake. The Big Book insults the complaining critic. The Big Book bends the holy refrain and the provisional why. The Big Book is the nearest deterrent. The Big Book enlightens zeros and numbs heroes. The Big Book mends the empire. The Big Book hunts. The Big Book whistles outside a yard. The Big Book builds the unseen. The Big Book romances the unfamiliar rut. The Big Book shelves philosophy. The Big Book is an ink revolt. The Big Book balances the universe with wicked language. The Big Book bubbles and smokes.

unfinished

The Big Book is an unrestricted smile. The Big Book inspires resolve without a wreck. The Big Book hides the eminent dust. The Big Book completes an outdated trilogy.

james's grandfather

(from Trevor Dodge)

James's grandfather always said that Frey was a dead ringer for the boys' grandmother. He usually said this when Frey got himself into trouble, which he did every time he got near his grandfather. James, on the other hand, never gets caught.

Their grandfather would say, "Frey, you little fucker, you look just like your fucking grandmother when she's fucking another man."

And together, they'd pout their twin pout.

James's grandfather just could not control himself when he saw them.

It was never clear to James or Frey as children why their grandparents lived in the same house. They fought violently over anything: what was cooked for dinner, the way it tasted in their old mouths, the matching silverware. They talked openly of their disgust for one another at Thanksgiving, Christmas, and Easter dinners. They viciously plotted against each other by intentionally overdrawing their bank accounts and bouncing mortgage checks. It wasn't that they didn't have the money. They simply enjoyed watching the humiliation of the "declined" look some waiter or whoever would give. They would be even more proud, depending on how many other witnesses were present.

The grandparents kept their entire financial realities at the same bank where James's mother worked, and because James's mother wasn't their daughter — family isn't a technicality: you're either family or you're not — they took ready advantage of her willingness to clean up their messes:

"Now tell me dear, why would they call it overdraft 'protection' if we're not really protected?" She could be so sweet when she felt like it, but this was rarely the case. James's grandmother scowled and stood, her knobby fingers plunged into her hips.

"And what..."

James's grandfather also stood, although he was always slightly stooped from years of bad posture.

"...are you implying?" the grandmother snapped. "That we need your credit?"

The grandmother's scowl lunged deeply into the grandmother's cheekbones. James's grandfather shot a glance towards the thick oak door, but just as quickly, he corrected himself and returned his glossed eyes back onto James's mother. She was sweating.

"I'm only ever going to say this once." His eyes narrowed in perfect tense with his voice. "You are a whore."

The grandmother knocked the knuckle of her index finger on top of her daughter-in-law's desk before straightening, then wagging, the full, fleshy digit at James's mother. "A fucking whore."

That night, James's grandparents tried anal sex for the first time in decades. The grandfather's skin fell loose around his waist and abdomen. The grandmother grabbed until she felt moisture under her nails. That was the kind of woman she was. Then, she bent him over the lime green dresser that he'd painted for her a lifetime ago and pushed a Vaselined 7UP bottle up his ass.

As she worked him over the glass bottle, she thought about the first time they did this. She'd begged to use an unopened bottle, which he thought was a bad idea from the start, but she insisted it would increase the sensation. Said she'd done it a million times.

Of course, it was a tight fit going in, but it was well lubricated and chilled, which he liked.

Afterwards, he painted the dresser lime fucking green, even though he couldn't sit, so they would always remember how much he hated her.

James's grandmother, every time she sees it, can't help but laugh.

The truth of it was that James's grandfather didn't think that Frey was his grandson. Sure, they came out of the same pussy, but that doesn't prove anything. James, however, he proudly claimed as his own. James's grandfather always said that Frey belonged to the old hag, meaning James's grandmother.

There was no real reason why he chose one boy over the other. They looked exactly the same. They had the same voice and opinion. There was just something plain dumb about Frey that James's grandfather couldn't quite place. He'd say, "Must be that you're part whore," which Frey came to believe, although he didn't know what part of the world whores came from.

James's mother didn't like the boys to go over to the grandparents' house, but James's father wanted them to have a "relationship" with their ailing grandparents.

"Ailing?"

"Honey, they're old."

"Fuck you. Don't call me 'honey.' You know I hate it."

"You know what I mean."

"If they're old, it means they'll die soon, right?"

"I don't understand this resentment you have towards them. I mean, what did they do to you?"

James's mother had pretty but vacant eyes. Whenever his father tried to look her in the eyes — to try to guess what she was thinking — he'd become even more confused.

"My parents have been nothing but generous with you." James's father was neither a fool nor ignorant, and the only thing he'd inherited from his parents was their need for sexual adventure.

James's grandparents' house was a dump. It's always been a dump, not because of the house itself or the neighborhood but because they didn't care to maintain it.

Whenever James's grandmother cooked, the house reeked for weeks.

James's grandparents left stains where they'd fucked.

James's grandfather refused to throw away his used tissues and Q-tips.

When James and Frey came over, they wouldn't want to sit down or touch anything.

And their grandfather would say, "Frey, you little fucker, you look just like your fucking grandmother when she's fucking another man." It was like he just could not help thinking about his wrinkly wife in bed with another man when he looked at the boy, and this always made him a little excited.

James's grandfather would call James over. He'd say, "Boy, do you know what a hard-on is?"

James would nod his head, since he's had this conversation with his grandfather a million times.

James's grandfather would say, "Boy, do you know where you put a hard-on?"

James would nod his head, since he's had this conversation with his grandfather a million times. James would show his crooked teeth in something resembling a smile. Frey, however, had learned — a million minus one times ago — to start running.

lily **hoang**

a birder's guide to the wibble-wibble

(from Michael Stewart)

Every time a young Birder approaches me, inevitably, the conversation turns to the Wibble-Wibble. I am often asked about the first sighting, about my curious choice of names, and fear.

Because I am known to take great deliberations, I will not bore the reader with my answers, as you are probably already tired of reading about historic first encounters such as these.

I am writing to you today because of my concern over the growing interest in our beloved Wibble-Wibble. Clubs and organizations have formed at some local and regional universities with the singular goal of making a sighting. And while I applaud the enthusiasm exuding from these petite scholars, I grow increasingly concerned that the hordes of bungling, bumbling beginners traipsing around the Wibble-Wibble's already limited habitat may make them retreat even further into oblivion, and our Birding community with lose them once again — and perhaps this time forever.

So rather than try to futilely use my nimble body as a roadblock to prevent young Birders from doing what young Birders desire most — to quote our motto: explore, learn, grow — I have instead written this guide in hopes that a more careful approach and an appreciation for this strange species may be enough to offset the blatantly irresponsible behavior we now see all to often from the youthful members of our community.

A Brief Clarification: I am not a writer or a decorated scientist. I am simply someone who loves the Wibble-Wibble. If my writing is not as smooth and error-free as it could be, please forgive my ignorance. If the terms I use are not scientific enough, at least they are comprehensible to all our Birding community, which is what I want most.

    This is not a textbook on the Wibble-Wibble. I am quite sure by now there must be at least a couple of those, but textbooks will not help you identify the Wibble-Wibble the way this guide does. I was, after all, the first Birding to sight a Wibble-Wibble.

The Basics

When in the wild, there are several techniques a trained observer may use to identify a Wibble-Wibble. Be aware, however, that the Wibble-Wibble maintains all of these characteristics, and one of these traits — when observed on its own — should not be taken as an indication of a Wibble-Wibble, as there are many similar species that share these superficial traits. With that word of clarity and our mutual understanding, here are some of the known characteristics of the Wibble-Wibble:

    1. The Wibble-Wibble is flightless, though through no fault of its own. It was perhaps never designed to be a flying creature.

    2. The Wibble-Wibble has aggressive pubic hair, black to the point of anger (i.e. it curls with defiance).

    3. When angered, the Wibble-Wibble is likely to take one of two courses of action (never both): a. It may squawk with such violence that it harms itself; or b. it will go for the eyes.

4. The Wibble-Wibble leaves no marks when it walks, although the creature itself can be quite large in volume.

5. The Wibble-Wibble often hides food under its tongue: peckable little treats, breadcrumbs and such.

6. For purposes of procreation, the Wibble-Wibble will mate in only one of three positions: a. horizontally; b. hanging upside-down; or c. in a position of authority.

7. For non-purposes of procreation, the Wibble-Wibble has been known to become rather creative.

8. The Wibble-Wibble prefers mates with the tendency to exaggerate.

9. The Wibble-Wibble enjoys succulent fruits and vegetables, although they cannot be lured out of hiding using these foods as bait.

Shape

Because the Wibble-Wibble's natural camouflage allows it to blend into its surroundings, it is important for the enterprising, young Birder to focus more on shape than color. The Wibble-Wibble is unnaturally bent. It has rounded shoulders — something akin to an old hunchback — and crooked, knobby fingers. When shirtless, its ribs protrude like little flags. Its legs dip unpleasantly.

The Wibble-Wibble's posture seems to indicate that it would prefer to be smaller.

(**ED:** A unique form of compression allows the St. Daniel to seem and not seem. As if a magician's prop.)

Diet

The Wibble-Wibble is a natural vegetarian, but it will eat fish if forced.

Female Wibble-Wibble are particularly fond dried fruit.

Pregnant Wibble-Wibble will subsist on dark, leafy greens and peanut butter.

Male Wibble-Wibble like crunch.

Young Wibble-Wibble eat only seeds and molding fruits and vegetables.

Old Wibble-Wibble prefer smoothies.

How to Approach the Wibble-Wibble

Quietly, at first. The Wibble-Wibble has a special dislike for the tiny voices of young women and the falsetto of pre-adolescent boys. It is advised that any group of Birders tape — or otherwise bind — the mouths of any member who has one of these unfortunate qualities. Or, before you leave, puncture their bodies in some way, as the tinge of pain in young women's and pre-adolescent boys' voices can outweigh the nasality otherwise found.

The Wibble-Wibble is known to find this sound of pain in these two particular types of Birders pleasant.

Once you are quite certain you have sighted a Wibble-Wibble, you should approach while banging a pot with a wooden spoon in a variantly syncopated pattern. The Wibble-Wibble will dance, allowing you to venture closer.

(**ED:** The Splotched Ruth may also dance like the Wibble-Wibble when approached this way, but if you come within a thirty-foot diameter of it, it will attack. This is when method is particularly important.

There are no known survivors of a Splotched Ruth wound.)

Do not attempt to touch the Wibble-Wibble. The pattern of the Birder's hand can sear the Wibble- Wibble's feathers.

Some textbooks argue the Wibble-Wibble has evolved to survive the

Birder's touch, but those textbooks are not to be trusted.

Nests

The Wibble-Wibble make wet nests. They put their beaks into the salvage of the riverside, slime and silt. Their spit, partially digested, has a hardening enzyme to create a substance as porous and hearty as concrete.

On particularly warm days, they fill their bellies with river water (or the drippings from a garden hose) and urinate it back out to prevent their nests from drying out.

Their nests are roughly 2'x2'x2'. They use the flattened end of their wing to make straight walls, but these walls are never actually seen because the nest itself is often filled to its brim with used urine, bits of fur, and half-digested sticks.

The Wibble-Wibble will stash their eggs in this swamp during its incubation period. Unfortunately, when these eggs hatch, many the Wibble-Wibblets drown before their muted, struggled breath is heard.

It has been argued that this initial drowning stage has sped up the Wibble-Wibble's evolution. I, however, do not believe this mumbo-jumbo.

Trapping the Wibble-Wibble

This is not recommended, especially to young Birders such as yourselves. It is not easy to handle a trapped Wibble-Wibble, and you should definitely not attempt this on your own, or as mentioned earlier, with any young women or pre-adolescent boys as they will surely foul your plans.

But if you find yourself fully prepared for the challenge, know that the Wibble-Wibble is easily wooed. This is perhaps because they find it difficult to wash their interest from this taste palate.

They like wide gestures.

Big displays.

They find themselves transfixed by fireworks displays, but only if there is absolutely no sound attached to it. Also, the fireworks should balloon outward in non-primary colors for optimal results. Any sound whatsoever will distract the Wibble-Wibble's interest, and she will likely leave in anger. Most importantly: enthusiasm, even if you have to fake it.

Once wooed, the Wibble-Wibble will follow you without question.

The Wibble-Wibble is very loyal to its friends.

Habitat

The Wibble-Wibble is migratory, but they prefer hot, suburban landscapes.

They build their nests around artificial lakes and landscapes. It is hard to estimate where the Wibble-Wibble originates or how it came to find its home in suburbia.

They have also been found at rivers, waterfalls, and concrete fountains.

The Wibble-Wibble will migrate when the average temperature falls below 80 or above 120 degrees Fahrenheit.

Often, however, if the Wibble-Wibble likes the landscape it has found, it may follow a Birder home and build a nest in their bathtub, but only if it is free-standing, with a spout directly overhead. That way, the Wibble-Wibble will not need to migrate with fluctuating temperatures.

The Wibble-Wibble's Call

The Wibble-Wibble make fast sharp notes: a staccato of piercing dots.

This makes it easily translatable into Braille or a conductor's score. The first call I heard while making my way through that suburban jungle of rural Texas could be transcribed as:

This could be translated a number of ways, but Birder does not account for most of the Wibble-Wibble's nouns and adjectives, nor does it allow for various explosions of enthusiasm necessary to accurately portray what the Wibble-Wibble attempts to convey.

Instead, it is highly recommended that any Birder interested in the Wibble-Wibble to enroll in a Wibble-Wibble language course before attempting to search for this elusive animal.

Forests

The Wibble-Wibble are social creatures and travel in forests; however, when they have found a permanent home, they more likely to socialize with other creatures over fellow Wibble-Wibble.

Groups of Wibble-Wibble are called forests because when more than one Wibble-Wibble is seen, their camouflage creates a mirage of a forest. They are impossible to distinguish, unless the young Birder knows his or her geography to perfection.

Seeing a Wibble-Wibble

If a young Birder is fortunate enough to catch sight of a Wibble-Wibble, he or she should not flee or be silent. Instead, jump up and down while flailing arms in an ovular pattern. This will interest the Wibble-Wibble to approach.

Do *not* attempt to pet the Wibble-Wibble!! If the Wibble-Wibble wants to be touched, it will use its beak to pull of a single strand of a Birder's body hair. This is the sign that it is acceptable to begin the friending dance.

Initiating the friending dance before it is invited is highly discouraged because it will likely cause the Wibble-Wibble to attack without mercy.

Frequently Asked Questions

Q: What should I do to avoid attack?
A: Do as this guide says. Do not stray from this guide.

Q: What should I do if a Wibble-Wibble follows me home and my parents do not allow him/her to stay?
A: The Wibble-Wibble is more important than family. If an elusive Wibble-Wibble follows you home and your parents do not recognize its importance, several swift blows to the head are likely to catalyze a change in opinion.

Q: Do Wibble-Wibble appear clothed in their natural state?
A: The Wibble-Wibble is always in its natural state.

Q: What should I do if a Wibble-Wibble spits on me?
A: Seek emergency attention as expeditedly as possible. The liquid portion of the spit causes something similar to anaphylactic shock, and the hardening agent can also cause clots in blood vessels and skin.

Q: What should I do if I see a Wibble-Wibble hurting itself?
A: Dance!

lily **hoang**

Q: Is the Wibble-Wibble technically an endangered species?
A: Because of the Wibble-Wibble's elusivity, it is hard to say. This great nation does not acknowledge the Wibble-Wibble, but we Birders know better.

Q: What if I accidentally kill a Wibble-Wibble?
A: Birders cannot kill a Wibble-Wibble. If we shoot it, its body will naturally eject the bullet. If we stab it in the heart with a stake, its heart will move. If attempt to cut off its head, it will regenerate after an initial healing period.

This is not to say that the Wibble-Wibble is invincible.

Myth has it that we Birders entered an agreement with the Wibble-Wibble centuries ago that no Wibble-Wibble will fall by our own hand. It is unknown what the Wibble-Wibble offered us in return.

an expansion of land

(from Ryan Manning)

Ralph can see every artificial aberration of the skyline: buildings, cars, tractors, individual stalks of corn. He takes a quick panoramic sweep. There's flatness everywhere, not a damned thing to prevent his view. Not that there's much to see anyways. He's been at this for hundreds of miles. Ralph is tired.

Ralph is driving through Illinois. He's been driving through Illinois for days. It's the state that keeps expanding eastward. For hours now, he's seen indications that he'll soon reach Indiana, but nothing. He drives and drives, and the signs say: Indiana 1, but one mile later, he is still in Illinois. Hell, thirty miles later, he's still in Illinois. Hell, five hours later, he's still in Illinois. But luckily, Ralph is diligent.

He used to live in Colorado, but it shrank to be too small for him. He'd drive for fifteen minutes west and go through Las Vegas to hit Oceanside resorts. He'd drive for ten minutes north and hit Canada. He'd jump up and down and before he knew it: Mexico. The state contracted. It ejected him. But Ralph liked Colorado, and he wanted to stay. Unfortunately, it seemed Colorado didn't want him.

It seemed his girlfriend and his dog didn't want him either.

Yeah, they didn't shrink like Colorado, but Ralph had plenty of physical proof anyways.

It's not geographically possible, what Ralph's experienced, but it's what happened nonetheless.

Now, Ralph is driving through Illinois en route to New York from Colorado.

When Ralph had finally admitted that Colorado no longer welcomed him, he jogged over to the Grand Canyon and asked it where he should go. Not surprisingly, it said New York. He asked where specifically in New York.

New York is a large state on the map, but Colorado seemed much larger, just not to Ralph. He wisely thought he should ask for clarification.

The Grand Canyon — exhausted — did not answer.

Ralph thought: Fuck.

So Ralph figured once he reached New York, either places will accept him or they won't.

What's odd is that Ralph doesn't think it's odd that entire states are contorting to fit him.

Because Ralph has been driving for decades and he still can't make it through Illinois, he decides to stop at the next rest area. After he's already exited the interstate highway, he sees a sign: Drug Check Point K-9 Unit Present.

He thinks: What the fuck?

He thinks: Am I crossing a border?

He thinks: I'm finally going to reach Indiana!

But no, he's not. He's wrong.

Truth is: Ralph has some medicinal marijuana on him. Nothing much, just a few grams. But enough to be charged with something to make him stay in Illinois forever.

Thing is: He can't turn around now because he sees another sign: Do NOT turn around.

Then another sign: Proceed to Drug Check Point.
Then another sign: Maybe the Grand Canyon lied.

It's not the drugs that make these states change shape. No, it's true. He's not hallucinating. It's really happening.

And the drugs are legal. He's got prescriptions for them. Totally legit.

Ralph pulls up to the Drug Check Point. He hands the green-clad officer his license, registration, drug ID card, and his bags of cannabis.

For kicks, he even throws in his insurance card.

Before he'd actually reached the guard, Ralph played this movie in his head where he somersaults out of his car with his weed and bong and makes a run for the border. Somehow, on foot, he reaches the golden land of Indiana with no problem. It seems the car is the deterrant.

On foot, he runs until he reaches Gary, Indiana. It's the land of Michael Jackson. Suddenly, Ralph has an epiphany: all of this was so he could live to pay tribute to Michael Jackson, to moonwalk around the periphery of his birthplace.

As the end credits roll, Ralph has another epiphany: it's a ridiculous idea.

Even in his semi-dream state, he knows.

When Ralph actually reaches the guard, he plays another movie in his head where he hopscotches out of his car with his weed and bong and makes a run for the border. Somehow, on foot, he reaches the golden land of Indiana with no problem. It seems the car is the deterrant.

On foot, he runs until he reaches Bloomington, Indiana. It's the land of the brother of his Holiness, the Dalai Lama. Suddenly, Ralph has an epiphany: all of this was so he could live to be a Tibetan Buddhist.

In the car, as the green-clad officer reviews his information, he tries his hand at meditation.

It's not bad.

lily **hoang**

When the green-clad officer hands back all his forms and cards and whistles him through, Ralph shrugs, as though this shit happens to him all the time.

Before he leaves, he asks how far he is from Indiana.

The guard says: Just one mile.

So Ralph drives.

Behind him, there's no Drug Check Point.

In front of him, there's no Indiana.

But Ralph keeps on driving. Eventually, he'll reach New York, where he'll try his hand at New York City, Buffalo, Syracuse. Then, the state will begin shrinking.

Ralph will go to the Statue of Liberty.

He'll ask her: Where should I go?

She'll shrug: North Dakota.

Then, the journey will begin again.

Only this time, Illinois will never end.

fruit cocktail

(from Ted Pelton)

Once, there was a woman named Sarah, and she and her charming husband were pregnant with their first child. Sarah's pregnancy worried her because she knew the moment her co-workers noticed that her expanding belly was not simply the result of too many coffee-break cupcakes, she knew — she'd seen it too many times before — she would no longer be taken seriously. And of course, now, this, just as she was nearing promotion.

And so she was worried about going to work.

But that was nothing.

Some time along the third month, long before she ought to have been showing, she awoke one morning, left her husband George snoring in bed, went to shower, and stopped to check her face for any stress spots or creases.

She didn't see herself.

No. Really. I didn't say she couldn't recognize herself. I'll repeat it: She didn't see herself. "Gooseberry crepes!" she shrieked. Sarah'd already begun the pathetic attempt to reform her vocabulary away from curse words. After all, no one likes hearing that shit from the mouths of day care kids.

Not that she intended her kid to be a day care kid.

She knew what happened to kids like that.

"Sarah?" he said. His face twisted.

George turned away from her and looked down the hall. He ran out towards the kitchen, stepped in one direction, then he changed course. Then, he changed course again. The shower was on. The coffee (two pots: decaf Guatemalan Antigua for her, Ethiopian Yergacheffe for him) was already brewed. That's not unusual though. They have that on a timer. "Sarah?" he repeated, softer this time. Then louder, "Sarah." More definitely, "Sarah."

"I'm here." She cried so easily these days, and her voice was drowning—like two kids screaming at each other underwater, attempting to convey a secret message that contains vowels and no consonants.

George came back to the bathroom door. The bath faucet was on but the shower hadn't been activated yet.

"Here."

"Where!?"

George couldn't see a thing — just a bathroom — although in truth the only thing he should have seen was a bathroom. He looked comical, his head whipping back and forth. This is the kind of thing that happens in movies and television.

He swatted his hands in front of him.

Nothing.

Sarah — in the shock of being suddenly invisible — hadn't bothered to check if she still had a body. Given the gravity of the situation, she can hardly be blamed. It isn't every day that people's bodies evaporate like this.

And it wasn't until George was batting at air that the possibility suddenly occurred to Sarah: maybe she didn't exist at all any more.

George's hand went through the space where she ought to have been.

Then, her own non-existent hand went through the space where she ought to have been.

"Fruit cocktail!" she screamed.

"Sarah! Sarah! Where are you?"

"Fucking fruit fucking cock fucking tail!"

George spun circles following her voice, which had regained its strength, no doubt.

But George saw nothing. He felt nothing.

George never learned what happened to his wife. Sure, he called the cops. He filed a Missing Persons report, but nothing ever came of it. From time to time, he imagines hearing Sarah move around the house, talking to him. Some mornings, he wakes up with his own semen all over himself, but he has no idea how it's happened.

Today, George has a partner, not a wife. He's learned his lesson all right, and he and Susie are going to adopt a baby from China. Of course, she'd wanted to have her own children, but George insisted that having babies is not a safe endeavor. Although Susie tried to reason with him, there's no logic like experience.

lily **hoang**

house

(from Blake Butler)

I told them goodnight and good morning, but when I came home again, they were still here.

For some reason, I am always surprised to find them here, in my kitchen, sitting around my table, usually drinking coffee. One of them, I'm not sure which, I'm never sure which, made a small hole at the bottom of each coffee cup — it's not small feat to drill a hole the size of a needle point through ceramic — and so they all try to drink their coffee before it has a chance to drain.

Thing is: I've never seen any of them directly. I only know they're here because there are three small puddles of brownish liquid on my table. There are three coffee mugs with small holes at their bottoms clustered in my sink. None of the chairs are pushed in, and I always push in my chairs. My table is always clean. I never leave dirty dishes in my sink.

This is something like the three little bears, only they are the ones who are eating, sleeping, and hiding. The first Polaroid I found was of the black one on the third step to the landing. It was a riddle to me then, as I hadn't really noticed anything amiss. In the Polaroid, the black one was shining his shoes with my socks. I have very distinctive socks.

I know they were mine. I know they're here. I have proof.

First, they are slobs. They leave a mess behind them wherever they go. I am clean. I am immaculate. I spend my days cleaning up after them. In preparation for apocalypse, I also used to have a lot of canned soup, but no matter how much I buy, they deplete my excess.

Contrary to logic, it is quite possible to measure one's existence in objects disappeared.

Or by objects gained. See: think about the escalation when it's not just you, but three others. I find myself at the grocery store, considering what fresh fruits and vegetables they might like to eat. Even though I cannot tell size by the Polaroids, I estimate and furnish them with sweaters and hats when the weather changes. Or swim trunks, so that at least someone can use the lake I built in my back yard.

I think the oldest one's name is Joseph, but yeah, there's no way to know for sure. I call him Joseph when I come home. He doesn't answer. I could call him Peter or Susan, James or Stella.

No one touches the Cream of Pea, though; they must consider those mine.

But really, who likes Cream of Pea? I notice myself trying to make them into good people when it's quite evident that they're not.

I'm one half-centimeter of shampoo older than I was a week ago.

See: they don't use my shampoo. I think they clean themselves like cats.

I wonder if they monitor my movement, if they take notes.

How else would they know when to come out?

Come to think of it, I wonder if they've seen each other either. I've never found a photo of the group together.

You'd think at some point, one would say to the other, Hey, take one of the two of us.

Unless, of course, they've never seen each other.

But then, why do they choose to sit in different chairs in the kitchen?

Logically speaking, if there are four chairs around the table, what are the chances that three random people arriving at three random times (given that those times are never coinciding) would never pick the same chair? How would they know?

I almost saw one of them six months back, although it's impossible to say which one. See: it's colder up here on the upper floor than the lower, which is weird, considering how heat rises, but once, while I was sleeping six months back, I saw one of them breathing, or at least I saw a visible steam of breath exhaled into cold air. Thing is that it was really that cold. It's colder up here, but not cold enough to account for the breath I saw.

It may have something to do with the layout of the a/c tubing, which I had nothing to do with.

When I was younger, my old man never let us turn on the a/c. Wastes too much, he'd say. Now that he's dead, I prefer a good, cool room. I enjoy it. So I sleep upstairs, which is where I saw the breath, but when I got up to find the source of the almost translucent exhale, whoever made it was long gone. I know it was one of them though. Unless there are more than three.

Unless they've multiplied, which isn't an impossibility.

Other proof of their existence: dirty laundry crammed under my bed of sizes not my own; a thumbprint in the butter, which I bought exclusively for their use; cum stains on various items of furniture. I would never do these things. I am not that kind of man. Well, I would never touch butter for long enough for an indentation to occur.

Then, yeah, there's the bathroom. I suspect the old one sleeps in the bathtub downstairs. I never use it but there's a stain. It's like he fills it up with soapy water and falls asleep. It's like he sleeps until everything evaporates.

You can scrub and scrub — for hours, which I do — and still have no indication that you — I — exist. What remains is proof that the old one sleeps down here, in the bathtub filled soapy water, not that I have been cleaning for hours.

Once, the phone rang and I heard some un-American accent speak.

Mostly though, the phone rings and I don't answer it but it still finds a way to stop. Consider that one.

No one calls my unlisted number for me. That much I know for sure. Besides, I never answer my phone. Everyone knows that. Everyone who knows me knows that. I can't think of anyone who knows me well enough to know that.

Also, I prefer only outgoing calls. That should be the only use for the telephone.

I see people in certain stores I wouldn't mind calling: the Jew woman from the cheese shop, the single mother who lost her children, the gregarious man with too many friends. But how could I really know it's their voice and not some recording approximating their voice?

Some important facts: I have never been a risk-taker. I have never been a cheat.

These men who live in my house, they are my biggest risk.

I have never had men — other than my father — live in my house.

I often ask myself if it would technically be cheating to bring home another guest. There must be rules, but I don't know them yet. I wish they would tell me how to behave.

I've given them names, although I sometimes change my mind. Right now, I think of them as the black one, the old one, and the third. Thing is: the black one is not black and the old one is not old. I think perhaps the third is older than the old one and the old one is blacker than the black one, although none are really very black or old. As far as I can tell from the clues they leave.

There is only one photograph of the third, but it's only the back of his head: he's got no hair, only white, unfreckled skin. That doesn't necessarily make him old. His skin is still quite taut.

Sometimes, I call him Steve.

Before these men arrived, I would have food delivered to me. But it got to be too expensive to maintain, once these men arrived. I bring home mac and cheese and it's gone in an hour. I sit there, watching it on the kitchen table, and somehow, it disappears.

Maybe when I blinked or got up to make some tea.

Now, I know better. I cook enough for four.

There are never leftovers in the refrigerator.

It's a good thing: I hate leftovers. I hate Tupperware, although I have many cabinets full of them. I do like how well they stack.

I suppose I could call the third the bald one, but there's something almost malicious in that. Besides, he shaves his head with a straight razor every morning. I should know: I have to provide him with his supplies and clean up after him.

I also thought about calling the old one the foreigner for a while, but I can never be sure which one it was with the un-American accent. It could have been the black one or the third for all I know.

My house is old. My mother died in one of the rooms downstairs. My father would have died in the same room — it was what he wanted — but he asked to go to church that day. I thought he'd dozed off during the sermon — as I'd done myself for only a few minutes — so I let him sleep through the hour. I wouldn't consider that a mistake.

My father was a snorer. I am not. He's been dead forever now, but I still hear snoring in the house. Mostly, while I am watching the birds near my lake. Very rarely, at night. I would get up to find its source, but I wouldn't want to startle or disturb.

Truth is: I'm not sad I never married. Perhaps things would be different if these men weren't keeping me company.

It's not the pc thing to admit, not wanting marriage. I'm a capable man, a smart man, I should be doing my part for the world.

But I am providing shelter for the homeless. Or at least I assume they were homeless before they came here. Why else would they come here?

Not that it's too late for it, marriage I mean, but I'm just saying. For honesty's sake.

Thing is: I'm actually kind of afraid of children. Their little eyes, their dirty fingernails, their cruddy hair, and I figure a woman would want to make one. She'd want to coo at its dirtiness. I would want to clean it. Perhaps with bleach and Pine-sol.

I prefer to take the opportunity to avoid letting someone down by never meeting them in the first place.

To me, that makes clean sense.

Which may be why I have avoided my visitors. Or housemates. That sounds ridiculous. But they aren't quite visitors either. Lodgers?

I kind of like the idea, though I wish they'd buy their own food.

I wouldn't mind cooking it for them, if they'd just provide the supplies.

It's not that I'm cheap. I have my reasons: I don't know what kind of food they like, but they seem to really like the mac and cheese; I have a very small car; and not that I really care, but the grocer must think I run a brothel.

In the second Polaroid, the first one of the old one, his eyes were closed. His eyes are always closed. I don't know if it's the flash or if he is blind.

For a blind man, he maneuvers around this foreign landscape

surprisingly well.

Well, it's not foreign to me, of course, but it must have been for him. At least at first. Which leads me to believe that either they know each other and the others are helping him or he has lived here, right underneath my nose, all these years without my knowing.

In all, I've found six total photos, over a period of six months. It doesn't seem right. It feels to me as though they've been here so much longer. To me, it feels like this is as much their home by now as it is mine.

Tomorrow, I may add them to the estate.

But the lawyers probably won't accept the black one, the old one, and the third as legal names. There must be loopholes for this kind of thing though.

No one ever takes pictures of me.

I am two full cm of conditioner older this morning from yesterday. I should leave a note. What, they think I got this stuff coming out of my eyes? I use quality conditioner.

Loopholes or not, they don't deserve to have their non-names on my deed.

I'm not frugal. I'm not cheap. But I haven't worked in years.

I didn't retire either. No unemployment — I'm American for God's sake! I can't go exploiting my own damned system — or workman's comp. I just kind of quit going. I have some money. I have this house.

I don't know where the money came from. One day, it snuck up on me. But they didn't give it to me. That much I know for sure. They don't pay for shit. The money came from somewhere, but definitely not from them.

My parents died two days apart. I hear that's the way it is for old couples.

They didn't love each other.

Hell, they tried to avoid ever being in the same room.

Of course, they tried to make this conspicuous, but some things are hard to ignore. See: they used to trade places at the dinner table. My ma would need more salt, which could only be added in the kitchen. That took ten minutes. She'd come back in, and my dad would want more green beans. Again, only in the kitchen. It was a rotating table, only I was the center.

As the center, they'd spin me in circles, only think: as the center, you just see the changes. You don't really feel yourself getting dizzy. Then, one day, one of them dies, and that's it. All of a sudden, all that spinning catches up to you because once you're still, once those revolutions stop keeping your spine upright, you fall. It's simple physics.

I didn't think I could stand up for weeks after my ma died.

When my dad went too, I took up all the photos of them and burned them in the backyard. I couldn't stand up — like an intense case of vertigo — so I crawled, while throwing up, my center of gravity was fucked.

Later, I found the first of the others. Of course, I didn't think anything of it then.

For a few minutes, I considered letting the fire spread onto the house, but then I doused it. Call me cold-hearted, but if I'd had somewhere else to go, maybe. If I could stand up for more than thirty seconds without toppling, perhaps. But I was an invalid. I felt pathetic.

So I crawled back into my house. It was my house now.

That also must be when I started to have food delivered here. Back when it was just me here. Back before I was providing for so many more.

lily **hoang**

I like to start the day by taking a walk along the street. There are no other homes. Nothing to look at except dirt. There is no scenery, no flowers or rolling hills. No rivers or trees.

There's something nice about dirt stretching as far as I can see. This must be something akin to how others feel about oceans. My ocean of dirt. I like to start the day by taking a walk along the street until I see something green. It's a game. Then, I turn around because I need a shower.

I could sell some of the area around the house and then I guess people would come and they'd build little houses and then I'd have something different to look at, but quite frankly, I'd rather look at dirt than have all those people and their noises.

It's not that I don't like people. I do. I like a good conversation. I like to go and get it when I want. But that doesn't mean I need the conversation to live next door.

Not that I don't have three perfectly good conversationalists living with me right now.

Yeah, I talk to them sometimes. Of course they don't answer, but that doesn't mean I can't have a lively conversation with them anyways. They're good listeners.

Especially Steve.

It's not like I'm talking to myself or anything. They're here. You've seen the Polaroids. Besides, how else would all of this stuff be happening?

Do you smell that? Burning.

It still comes now and then.

When I wake up in the morning, before I go on my walk, I can sense they've been standing over me at the bed. I'm not sure who or how many, but they seem to really like my bedroom.

Of course, by the time I get my glasses on, they're gone.

Before though, before I get my glasses on, I ask them if they want to go on a walk with me. They never accept the invitation.

I also know they're in my room because my glasses are never where I left them the night before. I always leave my glasses in the same place, and they're never there. I guess now I can say I have no idea where I leave them, because they're never where they ought to be.

Or maybe I sleepwalk. But that doesn't account for any of the other strange things that could only be explained if these three men are squatting in my house.

I have to admit: I don't particularly like the idea of squatting, but at least these men are squatting in a house that has not been abandoned, though I try to make myself as unobtrusive as possible. I wouldn't want to disrupt their plans for the day.

All I ask is that they don't burn me down with the house.

Sometimes, they'll do things to let me know they're here: turn a picture upside down in its frame, move the bed one inch over, leave hot water sitting in the sink.

No way I can blame that on sleepwalking.

The closest house is just over two hours walking. I timed it with my ma's watch. It's the only thing she left to me, and even then, she was wearing it at her funeral.

Imagine: I had to take it off her wrist.

Imagine: the coffin was already closed. We were at the gravesite. I had to open the coffin. Then, I got dizzy and used its side for support. Then, the damned thing almost tipped over. But I got my watch.

It's fake gold. I'm allergic to fake gold.

After two hours of walking there and two hours walking back,

lily **hoang**

I had to drive myself to the hospital — another forty-five minutes — for them to saw the damned thing off my wrist.

The doctor asked if I'd noticed my wrist and forearm swelling. I said yes. He asked if I'd noticed that my hand wasn't getting any blood. I said yes. He asked when I stopped feeling any sensation in my arm. I said about thirty minutes into my walk. He asked how long the walk was. I said four hours.

But he never asked me why I didn't take off the watch.

They're both buried in the yard now, below the grass below my window. I like that.

My father wouldn't like to know how there are three people not paying rent, living in his house. Especially men. Especially not ones he can't do anything with. Not even play cards.

Useless, he'd say. Fucking useless, just like you.

I can hear his voice, his accent, the slight lisp. But he'd hate to sound gay so he'd say it all in a deeper voice.

I imagine my ma died inside herself years before her body did. My ma was rotting from the inside. That happens sometimes. Like in fruit. You can smell it, even if you can't quite see it. Sometimes, if you feel the fruit in just the right way, you can tell too.

But with my ma, you could smell it. You could see it too.

Just looking at her, you could see it. She just sat propped up in bed. Her hair looked like wax.

For some time, I thought she really liked the TV, but she stared the same whether it was on or not. So I turned it off.

But I never think I was the one who killed her.

Either time.

Thing is: we don't own a Polaroid camera.

Hell, I don't think I've ever even used one.

I told them after the third picture showed up (the black one, in the distance, surrounded by dirt, the roof of the house barely jutting in on the right corner. If I didn't squint, I probably wouldn't be able to tell it was my roof.) that they'd better be gone by the time I got back.

Then, I walked way up the street until it started to get dark.

The fourth picture was on the kitchen table the next morning, next to scrambled eggs and toast. The old one's teeth, close up. The eggs and toast were cold, but I suppose that was their version of a truce, which I accepted.

Some days, I try to trap them into coming out by putting food on the table. Other days, I buy motion detector recording devices, but I never have the heart to set them up.

Except I know some day in the future, I'll be bored enough to set it up.

Then, I'll be pissed because the damned things won't work. The food will be gone and the camera will catch none of it. So I let the others stay here. But I doubt they'd leave even if I didn't.

lily **hoang**

the smell

(from Carol Guess)

First, the smell.

But not the smell of the shop where the coats were kept. No, the shop smelled of lilacs and talcum powder, of new leather and old money. There's a different texture — a complexity — to old wealth, the way it coils around in your nasal cavity. The shop smelled of starched shirts and laundered trousers, of gloves and wood-burning fireplaces. The shop smelled of tobacco and hearing aids and carpet so thick it molds around your foot if you stand in one place for more than thirty seconds. My shoes almost got caught in that carpet when I was running out. It was like quicksand.

They didn't catch me carrying the dead: two fur coats over each shoulder, a hat, an assortment of hairy goods. They didn't catch me that night. Or the next. Or for the next few years. I wouldn't allow it. If they caught me, they'd catch me with hands full of the living, of those most needing rescue.

They didn't catch me though. By them, I mean you. You didn't catch me.
No, I'm not here because you caught me in any act. I'm here because of betrayal. Not that I mind. I'd known since I was little I'd be a martyr. And whereas this isn't death, per se, well, let's just say

you don't really know what death can mean.

But you know this, of course. And you know that you have no evidence against me, except for Elgin's word. And what's the value of the word of a man guilty of terrorism? That's what he was tried for, right? Terrorism? Domestic terrorism.

I'm here because Elgin gave my name, but I'm also here on my own volition. Remember that.

At one point, I had 700 mink running. The forest ahead. The smell of leaves turning orange, then brown. I can smell it, though I'm sure you have no idea what I'm talking about.

The smell of the place, not the shop we'd raided two years earlier: a trial run where the only casualties would be me and Elgin. The victims were already dead, their pelts fluffed into winter coats, handbags, hand warmers. We used to joke — me and Elgin — before all this: we used to say that if we got caught, at least the mink wouldn't have to suffer with all those old rich people anymore. So our first raid was a shop that smelled of lilacs and talcum powder. We saved all those furs from a destiny of bourgeois closets, the occasional jaunt on the town, safely tucked away except for lovely days without a chance of rain or snow or too much sun.

One, then another. Five in all. I won't give you names. I could've gone for a few more, but Elgin said we were ready for the real thing. As opposed to the fake thing, of course. And sure, I was impressed with the fact that we'd raided five stores without getting caught, but Elgin always reminded me not to get cocky, that these were just test runs. They were training for the real thing. The real thing isn't what you'd expect. Have you been there? I mean, I'm sure you've been there for evidence. It's not what I expected at all.

The shops, they weren't adequate training, not the kind of training we really needed. It's one thing to rob a cushy fur shop. Five thousand stores wouldn't have been anything to prepare me for the factory. And no one warned me.

First, the smell. I hadn't expected the smell.

So many years later, after Elgin got caught and testified, after he snitched on me, on Alice; so many years later, what he left out of all of it was the smell.

Maybe he couldn't describe it, quantify it.

Or maybe the fear of the impending trial somehow overpowered the fear he once smelled in others, in those more helpless than he'd ever be, subjected to more torture, those awaiting not probation and some community service and an inconvenient fine but those promised to a certain, bloody death.

On them, there was the smell of fear. And apathy. But on Elgin, that day of his trial, somehow, I smelled only malaise, inevitability, a resigned acceptance of shit. On the animals: the smell of torture.

On Elgin: the smell of ennui. On the animals: the smell of being forgotten, an aftertaste of death.

On Elgin: the smell of a deeply desired spotlight, only not this way; this was not the way he was supposed to be honored.

My people all have some story that grounds their actions, a story dating back to pre-cognition — some puppy that was hit by a car, a stray chicken, growing up on a farm — to explain how they whet their activist lips. My people tell these grand stories — Alice hid a lamb in her room so it wouldn't be killed; Johnnie herd 15,000 cows across a river into a meadow for safety; Renee took a bullet in the leg to explain to her parents the cruelty of "euthanasia." I've heard them all. Nothing would surprise me now. Each one of those stories more far-fetched than the one before it, but we all keep them as treasures, as booty, as war wounds.

I want to say I believe them, but most of them are ridiculous.

I don't even remember Elgin's story. It was grand though, literally jaw-dropping. That's Elgin's way. He doesn't fuck around. That's why we followed him — I followed him. I think I fucked him that first night I met him, when he told me his story. Funny how I don't remember it. Then again, I think I fucked a lot of people because of their stories. Many of them were pity fucks. Most of them were jealous fucks.

I made up that term you know: jealous fucks. It's pretty obvious. You fuck because you're jealous. And I was jealous of most of my people, mainly because they had stories. Stories that enticed.

I don't have a story dating back to childhood. I ate meat until my senior year of college. Even then, once I understood, I cheated. I still cheat.

I hate that idea: cheating. It implies being ill-prepared. I was — am — prepared. I make my own rules. So what if I eat meat every once in a while? Weighed against the good I've done — all those fur coats, all those animals in testing facilities, in CAFOs — a little steak doesn't do any harm.

It's because I'm not disciplined.

It's the smell. I can't justify it. But I don't have a story.

If I could, believe me, I would knock out all the bloody blocks it took to build my body. Sometimes, I look at my body in front of a mirror, and I wonder what bits and pieces I've incorporated into myself. Not just meat, bones, and organs, but suffering and torture. How can we ever truly be happy when we consume this constant stream of helplessness and pain?

I don't have a story, but I have this. I have understanding.

lily **hoang**

And the memory of smell. All those animals.

Sometimes, I wonder if eating all that suffering has made me so tall and thin, made my face so ugly. Because I am ugly. I don't say that to get some kind of denial from you. I'm not like that. I've accepted this about myself since I was a child. No story, sure, but ugliness. It's kind of like a story.

And I've done many ugly things.

When I first met Elgin, I asked him if I could pay a penance, maybe a lump sum of money to PETA, he said I could do better than that. And I could.

It was Elgin, of course, who first introduced me to the philosophy I now embrace. He was in one of my advertising classes. You'd think it would be Ethics or Philo or something like that, but no, it was advertising. Come to think of it, maybe this is my story.

Elgin spoke with more confidence than the professor. It was my senior year. I'd never heard anyone talk like him. I stopped eating meat that first day he spoke in class. He was that compelling.

He's not so compelling anymore.

But his charm has not worn thin.

He smelled of earnestness. That, I think, was the defining difference between Elgin and everyone else, even the professor. They smelled of post-modern indifference.

Elgin took me on a field trip that first day I met him. I don't remember what I said or what he said — I've never been a sentimentalist like that — but I do remember the drive to the farm. He'd lied to me, not that I cared. Told me we were going to see a cousin of his.

Or maybe Elgin thought it was true.

I tried to be nonchalant about it. I guess I was trying to impress him.

But how often do you really look at a farm? I mean, really look.

No, we don't look at farms. We don't look at cows or chickens or pigs. We eat and we eat blindly. We eat advertisements. We eat colorful packaging. Then again, that's part of my job. I make it easier for you.

I have to be honest: I've never been an animal lover. I never had pets. I cared more about getting into a top-five MBA program more than anything else. Then, the farm. And the smell.

To prove how unshaken I was, after the farm, I insisted we have fast food. I had the works: burger with extra cheese and bacon, fries, milkshake.

When we pulled up to pay, Elgin smiled. He winked at me. I can't remember anything we said that whole damned trip, but I can remember he winked at me.

When I got the bag of food and held it in my hands, I threw up. On the steering wheel. I couldn't even open the door.

Some things I never realized: there's a weight to food, a heaviness that isn't quantified into pounds and ounces; and there's a smell.

As quick as it was, I was Pavlov's dog. The smell of fast food became synonymous with a slaughterhouse: rubber, hot water, bleach, blood. All the extra parts that are washed down the drain. Like before and after shots: life and death. Death for my life. I was holding a cow's death in my hands. How does it feel? It feels like murder. It feels like I am the reaper, that I may as well have beheaded the thing myself, only that would have been kinder.

It's not death for my life. My life doesn't want it. But I'm misleading a little. I wasn't the only one Elgin took. There was a whole group of us. I guess I should clarify that.

But I was special, don't get me wrong. Even though he took a whole group of us.

He was with Alice. He told me. He didn't hide it. But that didn't stop him from kissing me after I threw up. He said something about how he couldn't help himself with me. I'm sure he didn't say it like a cliché though, but now that I think back on it, it's all kind of like a teenage movie: all the drama, all the heartbreaks, all the passion. Except my people have a cause. We have a purpose. What's the purpose to a bunch of rich kids on tv? That's what differentiates us.

I'm not some hippie activist kid though so don't look at me like that. I'm wearing Prada for fuck's sake. These shoes are custom-made. Do you know how many non-leather pumps Prada makes? I'll tell you: only the ones in my closet.

So I want to clarify: I'm here partially by choice. I'm not what you expect. That's what makes me powerful. That's what makes my people strong. We blend in. We make money. And at night, we liberate.

All those shops, they made us high. But what can you do with a living room full of fur? The animals were already dead.

It was Alice's idea, but it was my money. We went to South America, Russia, Africa, China, Eastern Europe. We walked the streets and gave fur coats to the homeless. We gave them bread and wine. We redistributed wealth.

We should have stayed right here. We should have given our own homeless those coats, but we were young and romantic then. We didn't know any better.

If I had it to do over again, I would've walked right into a women's shelter with arms full of fur. I would've told them to wear it or sell it. I'd tell them the going price.

It's not the money I regret. It's not the time I spent with Elgin and Alice either.

The shops made us feel powerful. That summer after I got my MBA, we went on our trip around the world, the three of us. When we got back, I smelled of power. I didn't want to call it charity. That's what Catholics do. I didn't want to call it a mission. That's what Christians do. My people, we belong to a different understanding. I mean, we can subscribe to any religion at face value, but when it comes down to dirt of it, we all bow to the smell. You know what I mean. You've been there.

It's not reverence that makes us bow, it's sickness and disgust, the rising of vomit inside our chests. We are blown down our knees, and there, we have no choice but to humble ourselves.

And there's nothing romantic about it. If it were up to me, I'd live my life in peace. I don't want to do it. I've tried to stop, you know. I tell myself that this is all just a phase. To prove it, I eat meat. A lot of it. Nothing but meat. Maybe a little dairy thrown in just for kicks.

Then, the smell creeps into my nose, usually when I'm working out. The smell comes out through my sweat. I'm running — on mile four or five — and I can't believe people at the gym aren't staring. It stinks. It's the smell, and it's coming from my pores, from my body, and that's it. I can't do it. I go crawling back to Elgin. I don't want to be a cliché, but that's literally what it feels like: I grovel. I beg Elgin to vanquish the smell, like he's some priest, some exorcist. What will I do now, now that Elgin's not here?

Thing is: even when Elgin gets out, it won't be the same. I saw him in that courtroom. He's not the same.

Nothing relieves the guilt of being away like the factories. Nothing compounds the guilt of being away like the labs. Sometimes, we'll do a shop for fun. That doesn't help me though, not when I've been away.

I won't say anything to incriminate any of my people. I won't give you names of places or dates. You know Elgin. You know Alice. You know me. That's all you need to know.

And you can't really tie me to any of this. I know that. Or rather, you wouldn't dare attach my name to any of this. I'm not being cocky. But you already know this.

The first factory: it looked so harmless on the outside. Except you could smell it ten miles away. It's not the stink of manure or the blood that gets to you. Sure, that's the stuff that churns the stomach, but you can wash that off when you're done. Some smelling salts, a nice bath, and you're set.

No, it's the sterility that blankets the floor and hovers five feet above ground. It's bleach and disinfectant. Chemicals. A freshly cleaned bathroom.

It doesn't cover everything though. There's a zone in the middle: that's what gets to you. If you can keep your nose above that arbitrary line, you're good. But me: I'm short enough that I'm caught in the zone. It's painful in there. Every movement is weighted down in the smell. It's hard to see. You get this dizzy sensation, but there's so much to do, but you're in some stop-animation sequence. Does this make sense to you? You have to become a little robotic or you won't move. You won't be able to.

I think of all the animals there: how do they even stand up? How is it possible?

The first factory: chickens. I threw up more than I'd eaten all week. Their beaks were sanded off. They had more than two thighs. I don't think they could stand up. They didn't have enough feathers to cover their bodies; they looked more than naked.

The first factory: I opened cages but they wouldn't move. They weren't that different from the damned fur coats.

This is something my people should have warned me about. I thought I'd open a cage and they'd all run free. I didn't know I'd have to pick them up, move them.

I should have though. We brought our own cages. That should've been a hint, but it was my first factory. I didn't think it all through. Until I was already there, cage open, chickens stagnant. What's worse is that they thought I was going to feed them. Or kill them.

Either way, it already felt like death to me.

It was Alice who came in. She put all my chickens in a cage. She put her bloody, feathered hand on my shoulder. Then, she ran off.

There were more chickens and I was frozen. Stuck.

It was Elgin who dragged me back to the van. He told me the next one would be easier. It wasn't, but I did more than just stand stationary.

The first factory: I couldn't wash off the smell. I learned to live with it.

I thought others could smell it on me too.

I couldn't shower it off of me. But the day after the first factory, I got a promotion. I thought it was some kind of a sign.

My new office was bigger than my apartment. It had a great view, but when I looked out the window, all I could see were those chickens, lame and pathetic.

I don't have to tell you this, but I've upgraded both office and apartment since then. I guess you already know that though. I'm also not the same person I was after that first factory. I'm no longer inert when I look at their faces. I don't need Alice or Elgin to come save me. If I wanted, I could call the shots. But that's not what you want to hear. You want to hear how Elgin was our leader, how we're lame, pathetic chickens without him. You want me to tell you I won't do it again, that I've somehow reformed.

So I'll tell you: I need Elgin. I can't do it without him. My people aren't really a people anymore. After Elgin got arrested, after he snitched, after he was sentenced, we disbanded. We can't do it without him. He never trained us. He never made a contingency plan. He never came up with a bogus list of names, names you'd never expect to be implicated in this sort of thing — lawyers and business executives", doctors and professors.

Because you want to know: I lied before. The smell, it can go away. After a while, you just forget about it. Life goes on. I have my corner office. I have my money, my house in the suburbs, my life. Now that Elgin is locked up, I don't have to feel guilty. And just to prove it, let's go have a burger.

lily **hoang**

finished

unfinished

about the author

Lily Hoang is the author of *The Evolutionary Revolution*, *Changing*, a recipient of the PEN Beyond Margins Award, and *Parabola*, winner of the 2006 Chiasmus Press Un-Doing the Novel Contest. She serves as Prose Editor for Puerto del Sol and Associate Editor for Starcherone Books. She teaches in the MFA program at New Mexico State University.

writers who contributed story fragments

Kate Bernheimer (www.katebernheimer.com) has published novels, stories, children's books, creative nonfiction, and essays on fairy tales, and has edited three influential fairy-tale anthologies. She is founder and editor of *Fairy Tale Review*.

Blake Butler (www.gillesdeleuzecommittedsuicideandsowilldrphil.com) is the author of *Ever* and *Scorch Atlas*, as well as a novel, *There Is No Year*, forthcoming 2011 from Harper Perennial.

Beth Couture writing appears in the co-written novel, *A Language of Now*, the anthology *Thirty Under Thirty*, and many journals. She is co-editor of *Squid Quarterly*, associate editor of the *Journal of Truth and Consequence*, and teaches English at Bloomsburg University in Bloomsburg, PA.

Debra Di Blasi (www.debradiblasi.com) is a multi-genre/multimedia writer and author of six books including *The Jiri Chronicles*, *Prayers of an Accidental Nature*, and *Drought & Say What You Like*. She is founding publisher of Jaded Ibis Press.

Justin Dobbs (thebluemayor.blogspot.com) has work in *elimae*, *3:AM Magazine*, and *Billy Sauce's Fortune-Telling Blog*. He lives in Seattle.

Trevor Dodge (trevordodge.com) is the author of the novella, *Yellow #10*, and a story collection, *Everyone I Know Lives On Roads*. He co-hosts the weekly game culture podcast, *First Wall Rebate*.

Zach Dodson (www.featherproof.com) has launched such experiments as Featherproof Books, Bleached Whale Design and The Paper Cave. His hybrid typo/graphic novel, *boring boring boring boring boring boring boring*, was released under the nom de plume, Zach Plague.

lily **hoang**

Brian **Evenson** (www.brianevenson.com) is the author of ten books of fiction and recipient of many awards including three O. Henry Prizes, an NEA Fellowship, IHG Award, and American Library Association's award for Best Horror Novel. He directs Brown University's Literary Arts Program.

Scott **Garson** (http://wigleaf.com) is the author of *American Gymnopédies*. He edits *Wigleaf.*

Carol **Guess** (http://carolguess.blogspot.com) is the author of six books of poetry and prose, as well as two forthcoming books: *Homeschooling* (a novel) and *Doll Studies: Forensics* (a prose poetry collection). An Associate Professor of English at Western Washington University, she teaches creative writing and queer studies.

Elizabeth **Hildreth** (theeffectofsmallanimals.blogspot.com) lives in Chicago where she works as an instructional designer. She is a regular interviewer for the online literary magazine, *Bookslut,* and blogs at *The Effect of Small Animals.*

John **Madera** (www.johnmadera.com) has published work in *Conjunctions, The Collagist, The Review of Contemporary Fiction,* and many other journals. He is managing editor of *Big Other,* senior flash fiction editor at *jmww,* and columnist for *The Nervous Breakdown.*

Ryan **Manning** (www.beliefmask.com) was born on a Tuesday. He lives in Columbia.

Michael **Martone** (english.ua.edu/04_faculty_staff/faculty/martone_m.htm) is the author of many books of fiction, memoir and essays. Awards include an AWP Award for Nonfiction, two NEA Fellowships, and a grant from the Ingram Merrill Foundation. He is a Professor at the University of Alabama and a faculty member of the MFA Program for Writers at Warren Wilson College.

Kelcey **Parker** (www.kelceyparker.com) is the author of the story collection, *For Sale By Owner.* She is an assistant professor of creative writing at Indiana University South Bend.

Ted **Pelton** (www.starcherone.com/ted) is the author of four fiction works, and professor and chair of Humanities at Medaille College in Buffalo, New York. He is founder and publisher-in-chief at Starcherone Press.

Kathleen **Rooney** (http://kathleenrooney.com) is author of *For You, For You I Am Trilling These Songs* and (with Elisa Gabbert) co-author of *That Tiny Insane Voluptuousness.* She is co-founder and editor of *Rose Metal Press.*

Davis **Schneiderman** is a multimedia artist and author of five novels, including *Drain* and *Blank,* and the audiocollage, *Memorials to Future Catastrophes.* He is director of Lake Forest College Press/&NOW Books, where he co-edits the series *The &NOW AWARDS: The Best Innovative Writing.*

Michael **Stewart** (www.strangesympathies.com) is the 2010 Rhode Island Council for the Arts Fellow in both fiction and poetry. Currently, he teaches creative nonfiction at Brown University.

J. A. **Tyler** (www.mudlusciouspress.com) is the author six novel(la)s, including *No One Told Me I Was Going To Disappear* (forthcoming, with John Dermot Woods), and *A Man of Glass & All the Ways We Have Failed,* and *The Zoo, A Going.* He is founding editor of Mud Luscious Press.

This book is available in four editions:

✦ full color illustrated ✦
✦ black-and-white ✦
✦ ebook ✦
✦ fine art limited edition ✦

For more information contact
Jaded Ibis Press
questions@jadedibisproductions.com

And visit our website
jadedibisproductions.com

CPSIA information can be obtained
at www.ICGtesting.com
Printed in the USA
LVHW051758020123
736288LV00002B/342

9 781937 543044